MC

DEA

DEATH AT THE VILLA

KATHERINE DALTON RENOIR ('Moray Dalton') was born in Hammersmith, London in 1881, the only child of a Canadian father and English mother.

The author wrote two well-received early novels, *Olive in Italy* (1909), and *The Sword of Love* (1920). However, her career in crime fiction did not begin until 1924, after which Moray Dalton published twenty-nine mysteries, the last in 1951. The majority of these feature her recurring sleuths, Scotland Yard inspector Hugh Collier and private inquiry agent Hermann Glide.

Moray Dalton married Louis Jean Renoir in 1921, and the couple had a son a year later. The author lived on the south coast of England for the majority of her life following the marriage. She died in Worthing, West Sussex, in 1963.

MORAY DALTON MYSTERIES
Available from Dean Street Press

MORAY DALTON

DEATH AT THE VILLA

With an introduction by Curtis Evans

DEAN STREET PRESS

FOOLS RUSH IN

Moray Dalton's *The Murder of Eve* (1945) and *Death at the Villa* (1946)

"I am John Bull to the background, yet I do want to see
Italy, just once. Everybody says it is marvelous. . . . ."
Caroline Abbott, *Where Angels Fear to Tread*,
E. M. Forster

For British novelist E. M. Forster, "Italy was to stand for
passion," observed American critic Lionel Trilling in his 1943
study of the author. Forster's 1901-02 tour in Italy with his
mother released the young man's smoldering creative fires,
resulting in the publication three years later of his acclaimed
first novel, *Where Angels Fear to Tread* (1905), the title
of which draws on the famous line from Alexander Pope's
An Essay on Criticism ("Fools rush in where angels fear
to tread") in telling the story of the consequences of free-
spirited widow Lilia Herriton's marriage in Italy, much to the
consternation of her straight-laced British in-laws, to Gino
Carella, a handsome younger man. Born in 1881, making her
just two years younger than E. M. Forster, British mystery
writer Moray Dalton (aka Katherine Dalton Renoir) likewise
must have toured Italy at some point in her youth around
the turn of the century, likely with her own mother in tow
for chaperonage. Her first published novel, *Olive in Italy*
(1909), which followed into print Forster's *Angels* by four
years, is the story of "an unconventional. . . . clear-sighted
girl who goes to Italy in a spirit of high adventure" and is
similarly suffused with Italian light and color. Recalling the
case of Lilia Herriton in *Angels*, Moray Dalton at Brighton

in 1921, three years after the death of her father and when she herself was just shy of forty years of age, married one Louis Jean Renoir, by whom she bore a son the next year, though the couple seems soon thereafter to have separated.

The bewitching spell which Mediterranean magic cast over Dalton is readily apparent as well in the crime fiction which she published from the 1920s through the 1940s, nowhere more so than in the novels *The Murder of Eve* (1945) and *Death at the Villa* (1946), a pair of uncommonly rich mystery thrillers that she wrote in the waning months of the Second World War. Doubtlessly Dalton was a confirmed Italophile, having during the previous World War even published poetry celebrating the martial heroism of Italy, the country having been, from the British perspective, on the right side in that conflict. How difficult it must have been for the author to bear witness to the terrible actions taken by Italians during the two decades when her beloved bel paese fell under the sway of brutally charismatic fascist dictator Benito Mussolini. Il Duce finally was summarily executed for his monstrous crimes by Italian partisans on April 28, 1945, merely a couple of months after the publication of *The Murder of Eve*. On February 27 of the *Liverpool Evening Express* had roundly praised Dalton's novel as "an imaginative thriller."

Excepting its epilogue, *The Murder of Eve* takes place four decades previous to its publication in the year 1905, perhaps the very year in which the author herself first visited Italy. It opens with a somewhat *Lady Chatterley*-ish shipboard romance between Roger Fordyce, an ingenuous British planter in Malaya returning home to visit his schoolgirl sister Penny and their spinster aunt, Polly Fordyce, at their home in Stratford-upon-Avon, and Nina, Lady Craven, a sophisticate who is on her way to Rome with her sickly husband, who is seeking medical treatment there. Roger and Nina meet for an assignation at the Albergo Del Castello, a once splendid but long-derelict villa located in a little town in the Apennines outside Rome that has been partially restored as a hotel by a handsome, ambitious, young Italian, Mario Laccetti, and his formidable sister Maddalena, whom we are told resembles Leonardo de Vinci's reputed Medusa. As the passionate affair—passionate on young Roger's part at least—burns itself out at the villa, Roger while wandering the grounds one morning imagines that he espies in a water tank a dead body, long black hair eerily afloat. When told of this by her lover, Nina objects to making any mention of it to local authorities, fearing exposure of their affair, and Mario later explains to Roger that the dead creature in the water tank was merely a mongrel dog. Roger and Nina part ways, with Roger returning to England, but the time which he spent at the villa ripples outward with fearsome consequences for himself and many others, both in England and Italy, including not only Penny and Aunt Polly, but disgraced *émigré* piano teacher Lily Oram (who recalls the title character in *Olive in Italy*); earnest British embassy official Ronald Guthrie; high-placed Italians Commendatore Rinaldo Marucci and Marchese Luigi de Sanctis; and British writer Francis Gale, his lovely schoolgirl daughter Anne and Francis' estranged ex-wife, the artist Eve Shandon. . . .

Reviewing the novel in March 1945, the *Plymouth Western Morning News* praised "the descriptions of life in Italy before the Great War," the in-depth characterizations ("The author is not content to outline his *[sic]* characters sketchily") and the "unexpected twist" at the end. Certainly *Eve* is an ambitious period thriller in a deadly serious vein, eschewing the stock formulae of the Edgar Wallace school of English shockers—works which seem, whatever their merits as popular entertainment, jejune by comparison. In *Eve* Dalton ironically has Roger Fordyce reflect, as he begins fumblingly in Italy to investigate what may be a case of murder (or murders), on the contrastingly comforting nature of the fictional stuff: "It was comparatively easy for the detective heroes of the thrillers he most enjoyed. They usually had the resources of New Scotland Yard at their disposal, or, if they happened to be amateurs, they had a faithful, though thick-headed, friend in attendance, or a valet who was also a boxing champion and an expert photographer."

Later in the novel the Marchese de Sanctis bracingly pronounces: "Poetic justice is so satisfying, but we live in a world of prose." *The Murder of Eve* is surprisingly modern in its refusal cheerily to tie up every loose end around a pretty, if predictable, package. Instead it looks ahead to modern crime fiction, where packages contain surprises—and by no means all of them pleasant ones. Yet the English characters in the novel remain stubbornly determined to try to do right as they deem it in Italy, whatever the dangers—and they are manifold—which may befall them. As one Italian character bemusedly reflects: "These English are a pest. Always poking their noses where they are not wanted. . . . . How is one to deal with such people? They are without sense, when you offer to buy they will not sell, they are hard when you expect them to be soft, and soft when you think they will be hard, and somehow by accident, they have acquired an empire."

Despite the menaces which "these English" face in Italy, Polly Fordyce—surely as formidable a spinster as *A Tale of*

Two Cities' Miss Pross, who braved France during the tumult of the Revolution—earnestly tells the Marchese: "I think you must know how much the English have always loved and admired Italy and the Italian people. I hope our countries will always be friends as they are now." Surely Aunt Polly was speaking as well for the author, whose John Bullish sentiments, typical of popular British authors of her day, invariably were softened by her warm Italian sympathies.

* * * * * * *

"All this blood and violence. God help us. It is like a bad dream. When shall we wake?"

Reverend Mother Superior at the Convent in the Via Due Macelli in *Death at the Villa*

THE second of Moray Dalton's Forties Italian mystery thrillers, *Death in the Villa*, takes place during the Second World War during the summer of 1943, when an Allied landing was imminent and the Mussolini regime teetered on the very brink of collapse. On the night of July 9-10, Allied forces launched Operation Husky, a successful invasion of Sicily, resulting two weeks later in the *25 Luglio* (the 25th of July), in which Benito Mussolini was ousted from power by King Victor Emanuel III and placed under arrest. On September 3, as the Allies launched an invasion of southern mainland Italy, the neophyte Italian government signed the Armistice of Cassibile, which declared a cessation of hostilities between Italy and the Allies. The publicizing of the armistice rapidly resulted in a German commando raid freeing Mussolini; the occupation of northern and central Italy by German forces; the establishment of the Italian Social

Republic, a collaborationist puppet state nominally headed by *Il Duce*; and the beginning of the nearly twenty-month Italian Civil War, during which German forces committed numerous atrocities against the Italian populace, resulting in thousands of civilian deaths.

Turbulent and terrible times indeed, and Moray Dalton dramatically captures their early days in *Death at the Villa*. Like much of *The Murder of Eve*, *Death at the Villa* is set at an old country mansion in the Apennines, this time the Villa Gualtieri, ancestral home of the Marchese Gaultieri. While the widowed Marchese occupies himself in Rome with his accommodating mistress and other dilettante interests, his country villa is occupied by his widowed young daughter-in-law Chiara (her husband Amedeo, the Marchese's son, recently went down in his plane over the Mediterranean, six weeks after the birth of their child) and her young companion and poor relation Alda Olivieri, both of whom are under the supervision of middle-aged widow Amalia Marucci, a vague distant cousin whom the Marchese took in, along with her implicitly gay son Silvio, an ardent Fascist, after the death in Venice of her husband Ettore. (Could Ettore Marucci have been a relation of Commendatore Rinaldo Marucci from *The Murder of Eve*?)

Alda's quiet, recessive country life is disrupted when buxom local farmer's daughter Marietta Donati reveals that her family has taken in a wounded English paratrooper. With the help of a kindly local priest, Don Luigi Cappelli, Alda shelters the handsome Englishman, Richard Drew, in an abandoned Etruscan tomb, all the while attempting to evade the prying eyes of Amalia Marucci, who is eager, for purposes of her own, to discredit Alda and evict her from the villa. Soon, however, Amalia's wicked machinations bear poisonous fruit, as the war inexorably closes in on them all. Can a stalwart young Englishman come daringly to the rescue of a fair damsel in a tumultuous foreign land where he himself stands in need of rescuing?

Death at the Villa is unique in the genre in coupling private murder with public terror. (In terms of subject matter I am reminded of British crime writer Michael Gilbert's innovative 1952 novel *Death in Captivity*, a mystery, drawing on the author's own personal experiences, which is innovatively set in 1943 in an Italian prisoner-of-war camp.) It makes, to my mind, gripping reading, with the last third of the novel in particular constituting the essence of the term "page turner." A contemporary review compared *Villa* to "classical Italian opera," avowing that its "narrative of jealousy, violence, tragedy and innocence against a somber background" made for "convincing and gripping reading." More recently the late crime fiction connoisseur Jacques Barzun praised the novel's "tense situation, beautifully plotted and narrated," and its "admirably diversified characters and . . . picture of the times."

For my part I was reminded, when reading *Death at the Villa*, of the dark French television wartime drama series *Un village Français* (2009-2017). I imagine that *Villa* would make a similarly compelling television production— as would, for that matter, *The Murder of Eve*. In both of her non-series Forties Italian crime novels Moray Dalton clearly aimed to take her crime writing in a more realistic and relevant direction, one where murder really matters. In this I believe she succeeded admirably.

Curtis Evans

Chapter I
ENTER RICHARD DREW

Since the fifteenth century the Donati had been charcoal burners on the Gualtieri estate, which included a large part of the chestnut woods that covered the mountainside. The little stone-built podere stood in a clearing.

The Donati grew enough maize for their own needs and had a few olive trees and vines. Their hereditary link with the family of the marchese was a close one, for, whenever possible, a woman of the Donati served as foster mother to the children born in the Villa. For many generations, wives and daughters of the charcoal burners had been able to remember a few months in comparative luxury in lives that were otherwise hard enough. But Marietta had made a break with tradition by refusing to leave her parents, who were old and needed her, and the young marchesina, whose health had given cause for anxiety since her husband's plane had been lost on a night patrol over the Mediterranean six weeks after the birth of their child, had been persuaded to part with him for a few months.

It was nearly two miles from the Villa to the podere, a steep uphill climb by a rough foot track, and Chiara was short of breath after walking a hundred yards, but she must know how her baby was getting on, so her cousin Alda went up instead of her, two or three times a week.

The marchese had given orders that his daughter-in-law was not to venture beyond the grounds of the Villa without a suitable escort, but Alda might do as she pleased. She was a poor relation, an orphaned cousin of Chiara's who had been brought up with her and had been offered a home at the Villa by the marchese, who saw that Chiara needed the company of a girl about her own age.

Alda enjoyed her visits to the podere. Life at the Villa was too restricted and uneventful for her, though she loved her cousin and was glad to be with her, and she welcomed any break in the monotony of her days. The baby was thriving, and Marietta was obviously devoted to him. Alda often found her sitting on the stone steps that led to the upper floor of the podere, looking like a rustic madonna, placid and serene, with her nursling asleep on her knees. One could not imagine a more complete contrast to Chiara's exquisite fragility.

Marietta was a humble creature, completely illiterate, never leaving the podere, except when she went down to the town of Mont Alvino with her old father to sell their charcoal. On these occasions she always spent a few soldi on candles to burn before one of the altars in the Duomo for her husband, who was a soldier fighting somewhere far away. It was many months since she had heard from him, but Domeniddio would take care of him, and meanwhile she had the marchesina's baby to console her for the loss of her own.

One afternoon in early summer, Alda left the rest of the household at the Villa enjoying their siesta, and climbed the hill to the podere. It seemed an afternoon like any other, and she had no idea that she had reached a landmark in her life.

It was comparatively cool in the shade of the woods and there was no sound but that which never ceases throughout the Italian summer, the drone of a million grasshoppers. Alda climbed steadily without lingering as she sometimes did, to pick the anemones that starred the scanty coarse grass. As she came out of the wood into the small clearing about the podere she saw Marietta coming from the spring with her copper water-pot on her head, and waved to her.

Marietta reached the foot of the stone flight of stairs that led up to the living-rooms on the first floor. The splendid muscles of her bare brown arms rippled as she set the brimming pot down and turned, smiling, to greet the visitor. There was a child-like admiration in her dark eyes as she said *"Che bellezza, signorina—"*

Alda was wearing one of her cousin Chiara's cast-offs, a sleeveless frock of pale pink washing silk. Her wide-brimmed hat of Tuscan straw shaded the small face with the pointed chin, pert little tip-tilted nose, wide generous mouth and clear hazel eyes, a face which la Marucci did not hesitate to describe as brutta, and which even her friends might call more piquante than pretty.

To Marietta, however, she was the glass of fashion and the mould of form, and Alda, who down at the Villa was of very little account, was human enough to enjoy the impression she made on the simple folk at the podere.

"How is the baby?"

"I think a tooth is coming through. He is well, though. He is asleep in his cradle in my room. I will fetch him presently. How is her excellency, the marchesina?"

Alda sighed. "Very nervous. Full of fancies, full of fears."

"What has she to be afraid of?"

"Something, perhaps," said Alda slowly. "I am not sure." She could not explain the sense of oppression that sometimes weighed even upon her down at the Villa.

Marietta had spread her shawl on the low wall on which, later in the summer, the crop of small yellow apricots would be laid to dry in the sun, and the two girls sat down side by side as they had done on many other afternoons.

The plain lay spread before them like a map, vineyards, fields of maize, white-walled farms, dark spearheads of cypresses, the grey-green of olive groves, and far away, the smoke of a train like a tiny feather blown by the wind. But there was no wind. The day was hot and still, so still that Alda heard a movement on the other side of the sunbaked house wall, against which she leaned.

The ground-floor of the podere was used only to store fodder for the donkey. The cow had been kept there when they had a cow, but she had died, and the goats were tethered in the open. The hens, too, were out, scrabbling in the dust.

Alda looked at Marietta, but Marietta was fumbling for her rosary in her apron pocket and did not meet her eyes.

Alda said nothing. It was the peasant girl who broke the silence between them. "Signorina, I want to show you something. My mother and I have talked it over. We agreed that you would advise us."

She took a large key from under a stone and unlocked the door of the cowshed. As the door swung open the man lying on a heap of dried fern by the wall groaned and turned over to avoid the strong light dazzling eyes weakened by days and nights spent in darkness.

Marietta filled a cup with water from the copper jar and, kneeling beside him on the rough stone floor, raised his head on her arm and held the cup to the bearded lips.

After a momentary hesitation, Alda moved forward, and stood looking with shrinking curiosity and compassion at the tousled fair hair escaping on either side of a dirty blood-stained bandage.

"Is he badly hurt?"

"My mother thinks not. No bones are broken, but he is bruised all over and his hands and knees are cut and scratched. He must have crawled a long distance. We found him in the woods when we were gathering fuel."

"How long ago?"

"Three days. He has been in a fever, muttering, crying out, sometimes even laughing. But we cannot understand one word. To-day he seems quieter and the fever is less. What are we to do with him, signorina?"

"If he is a German," said Alda in a hard voice, "his friends can be told and they can fetch him away."

Marietta lowered her voice and glanced uneasily towards the open door. "They told us the Germans were good people, but last winter foreign soldiers came up here and stole our pig and killed our dog. Mother had made me hide in a cupboard, but one of the men struck her when she begged them not to take our store of chestnuts, and they took her earrings of silver and coral, and the silver cross she always wore. Mother says she thinks this is an Englishman."

"English? There are no English here—unless he escaped from a prisoners' camp. There are none about here that I know of. But three nights ago I heard planes. What have you done with his clothes?"

"We buried them in the wood." Marietta embarked on a description of the stranger's clothing.

Alda nodded. "It sounds like the kit the marchesino wore when he was flying. But he may have baled out from a German machine. It is much more likely. I will speak to him. Perhaps he will answer."

Alda had learnt to speak both German and English at the convent. There had been two German nuns there and one English, as well as Mother Mary Aloysius from County Down.

She bent over the injured man, trying not to shrink from the stench of sweat and dried blood. Evidently Marietta and her mother had not attempted to wash him. They were well-meaning but ignorant.

"Are you feeling better?" she asked.

She saw then that his eyes, blue eyes, very sunken and bloodshot, were open and fixed on her face.

He said "Gosh. Have you seen a dream walking?"

The phrase was meaningless to Alda, who knew nothing of song hits. "Are you English?" she said.

"I am. Are you going to hand me over to the Jerries?"

"To what? I do not understand."

"To your German pals. The herrenvolk."

"I do not know," she said seriously. "It is difficult. But not to the Germans in any case. Besides, it is too late. It would get the Donati into trouble for not reporting at once to the authorities at Mont Alvino."

"Mont Alvino. We weren't so far out, then," he murmured. "Are the Germans there in force?"

"No. What should they do here? They pass through by train, or so I have heard, on their way to Africa."

"Africa!" he said. "You don't get the latest news here. Oh well, never mind. She—" he indicated Marietta—"she's been damned decent to me, and you look as if you might be inclined to give a chap a chance. If you'll give me a few hours' grace before you set your bloodhounds on my track I'll be obliged. I'll get going—"

He made an effort to rise, but sank back with a groan. "Sorry. I'm afraid I can't quite make it."

Alda was suddenly both frightened and angry. "I don't know why you should suppose I am a person who hunts men with dogs," she said, in her careful precise English. "This is not my house, and if the Donati give you food and shelter it is not my affair. You are quite safe from me. I shall say nothing at all."

She stopped, not sure that he had even heard her. His eyes were closed and his thin cheeks pallid. She turned abruptly and went outside, followed by Marietta. The peasant girl closed and locked the door and hid the key under a stone. "You are not angry, signorina?" she said humbly.

"Not with you. He—he seemed to think I would betray him."

"What would they do with him if they found him?"

"In uniform they are made prisoners of war. But he would be shot as a spy."

Marietta crossed herself. "God. help him, poverino. He is very young."

"Is he? I suppose so," said Alda absently. She was wondering if the Donati had realised their own danger. It was typical of their simplicity that they relied on her to advise them because she was a member of the household of their landlord and patron, the marchese Gualtieri.

"Listen," she said. "Keep him a little longer, but be very careful. I shall come again the day after to-morrow. I shall try to make a plan. I must go now, or it will be dark before I get back."

Supper, at the Villa Gualtieri, was usually served at half-past nine in the great dining-room, with old Pietro in his faded livery coat and wearing white cotton gloves, to wait at table.

The room was very large and lofty, with dim frescoes depicting the loves of Jupiter on the walls and ceiling. The windows were open on to the terrace and moths were always fluttering in to dash themselves against the shade of the old-fashioned oil lamp.

In the absence of the marchese, the distant cousin who had kept house for him since his wife's last illness, sat at the head of the table.

Amalia Marucci liked to be addressed as Donna Amalia, though she had no real right to that title. She was a woman nearing fifty, who flaunted the remains of what had once been dazzling beauty like a torn pennon borne out of the battle of her life. No one at the Villa knew what her past had been. She had written to the marchese a humble letter, explaining that she had been left a widow with straitened means and an only child, a son, who was delicate and needed care. The marchese had replied characteristically, offering her and her boy a home under his roof.

Gualtieri had never regretted his gesture. La Marucci was an admirable woman, efficient and discreet. She nursed the marchesa through the painful crisis of her obscure disease, and she ran the household more economically than that poor lady had ever done. If the servants disliked her that was to be understood.

The boy, Silvio, was perhaps less satisfactory. He was about sixteen when he arrived at the Villa, and the marchese had expected him to be younger. He was understood to be an ardent Fascist and usually wore the black shirt and breeches and smart riding-boots of a crack corps, though he was not strong enough to go in for any of the hardening exercises approved by the Duce; but apparently he was employed in some way by the Party, for he was often away for days and sometimes for weeks at a time. The marchese, who expected deference, got nothing more from him than an icy civility. In appearance he was almost girlish, with a slight willowy figure, a clean-cut face, with a skin of smooth ivory pallor, and very heavy-lidded blue eyes which he kept habitually half closed. The marchese's son, Amedeo, who was a few years older, had taken an instant dislike to him, though he never said so, and from the first the two young men had taken pains to avoid each other.

Silvio was away, and Donna Amalia sat with Chiara on her right and Alda on her left. It was a silent meal, for neither of the girls spoke unless they were spoken to, and la Marucci seemed to have nothing to say. Usually she addressed her remarks to the young marchesina, who always agreed with nervous haste to any comment she chose to make, and ignored Alda, whose presence she had always resented and whom she made a point of treating as a kind of upper servant. She and Chiara were both in the deep mourning affected by Italian widows, and Alda had changed her pink frock for a grey and white striped muslin. She was thinking as she ate her *pasta con pomodori* with the hearty appetite induced by her long walk, that if it were not for Chiara, who clung to her, she would not remain another day at the Villa. Her education at the convent had not fitted her to earn her living, but she supposed, with the vagueness of youth and inexperience, that there must be ways. The nuns seldom praised their pupils for anything but the dull virtues of docility, modesty, and humility, but the English nun, kind Mother Mary of the Angels, had once said, "You have brains, child, and, I think, courage and initiative, if you ever have a chance to use them." And on another less auspicious occasion the Irish Mother Mary Aloysius, after much head shaking, had ended with a reluctant grin and a "Sure, you dropped off a wagon load of monkeys."

Chiara had been different, always at the bottom of the class, but so sweet-natured and so lovely to look at that nothing else mattered. Alda, who was nearly two years younger than her cousin, had always felt much older and wiser, and took it as a matter of course that Chiara depended on her for guidance. Amedeo Gualtieri had taken the same view of her, as the sheep dog in charge of his ewe lamb. On his last leave of all he had said to her with unusual earnestness, "Alda, take care of Chiara and the baby. Watch over them."

Perhaps he had some premonition of his end. A few days later he was posted missing on a Mediterranean patrol, and ever since the Villa Gualtieri had been a house of mourning, and, for some reason not so easily explained, a house of fear.

Alda, raising her eyes from her plate, saw with some discomfort that Donna Amalia was watching her. Why? Was there anything different about her, anything to show that she had something on her mind? She hoped not. She knew that la Marucci disliked her. The idea of going away to earn her living lost half its charm when she reflected how pleased Chiara's duenna would be to get rid of her.

After supper the two girls sat in the little green drawing-room. Chiara was rather languidly at work on a little embroidered frock for her baby, and Alda was knitting a pair of tiny socks with pale blue silk. Donna Amalia left them, saying she was going to write letters. She glanced sharply from the golden head to the brown as she went out. "You are very industrious, my dears," she said in the slightly acid voice that the marchese never heard.

When the door closed behind her, Chiara dropped her work. "Why did she keep on looking at you?"

"You noticed it, too?"

"Of course. Why was it? Alda, there's nothing wrong with my baby? Nothing happened up at the podere? You would have told me—"

"Chiara, dearest, why will you torment yourself? Your baby is perfectly well. Nothing happened," said Alda firmly, and then thought "*Madonna mia*, that's a lie. But I must not tell Chiara."

She counted her stitches. Chiara, never a very ardent needlewoman, lay back in her chair, her thin hands folded, her bright hair gleaming in the lamplight.

"Play to me."

"Very well." Alda went to the piano, turned over an untidy pile of music, and played a Chopin Nocturne, not very well, but with a good deal of feeling. "I'm out of practice, but Donna Amalia hates to hear scales and exercises."

Chiara said dreamily, "When I married Amedeo I was so happy. We planned, when the war was over, to have an apartment in Rome and be by ourselves. That was all we wanted. Now I feel as if I had been given a life sentence, the Villa my jail, and la Marucci my jailer."

"Hush, Chiara, it would be easier if you could make yourself like her. After all, she saves you the trouble of housekeeping, and she is always civil to you."

"Contempt. That is what she feels for me," said Chiara unexpectedly. "I am stupid, but not so stupid that I can't see that. She despises me, but she hates you. I wonder why."

"You imagine things," said Alda, but she knew that Chiara was right. It was not pleasant to live under the same roof with someone who hated you, the thought of it was like something cold creeping at the back of your mind.

"I want to tell you something," said Chiara. "I think—I am almost sure—that I am going to have another baby."

Alda looked up at her quickly. "Oh, *cara mia*—are you glad?"

"Yes. I hope it will be a girl. Amedeo wanted a girl—"

Alda's eyes filled with tears. "Why did there have to be war," she said fiercely. "It was the Duce—" she broke off, biting her lips, and Chiara, who had turned pale, whispered *"Zitta!"*

Sheltered as their life was, they had heard what happened to people who said what they thought. Some topics were absolutely forbidden, some comments must never be made.

Alda recovered herself. "Does la Marucci know?"

"I haven't told her. I shall not tell anyone but you. Not yet."

Alda put down her knitting, went over to her cousin and hugged her.

It was as she went back to her place that she thought she heard a movement on the terrace. She went to the window and looked out. One of the garden chairs was drawn up close to the house wall, but it was unoccupied. Alda went to it and felt the cushion on the seat. It was quite warm. It was possible, she knew, that la Marucci had been out there listening. But could she have vanished from sight so quickly? Another explanation occurred to her.

Silvio's white Persian cat. The creature was always jumping up on the chairs and sharpening its claws on the furniture. Yes, it might have been the cat.

She rejoined Chiara, who was folding up her work. "Eleven o'clock. Let's go to bed."

Chapter II
LADIES IN WAITING

AT SEVEN o'clock old Caterina, the cook at the Villa, took a cup of black coffee up to Donna Amalia's room, and received her orders for the day. The ensuing discussion was apt to be prolonged, for the cook, who had been used to getting her own way with the late marchesa, disputed every item on the housekeeper's list, and la Marucci, who enjoyed thwarting her, allowed her to make her protests.

"Signora, it is too early for figs. I shall not find any in the market. The sugar should have lasted until the end of the week? Santissima Madonna! Has the signora forgotten the *zabaione* she herself demanded? One cannot make *zabaione* without sugar—"

At length some agreement was reached, and Donna Amalia opened her black handbag, which had snapping jaws like those of some small voracious animal, and doled out the marketing money.

"And do not waste too much time gossiping."

Caterina did not think this admonition worth an answer.

"The signorina Alda asks permission to go into the town with me."

"What for?"

"She wants to attend mass, and to make her confession if her confessor is there."

"Bene," said the other indifferently. "Tell her she may go."

When the old woman had gone out, grumbling under her breath, Amalia Marucci finished her coffee, slipped on her crisp white cotton wrapper, and went over to her dressing-table to begin a leisurely toilet. Her hair was long, thick, and jet black, and every morning she brushed it, or sometimes made the cameriera, Caterina's niece Bianca, brush it for twenty minutes, and while she watched her reflection and the rhythmic movements of the brush, she reflected on her past and planned for her future.

Amalia was a much more remarkable woman than the marchese had ever realised. Though she was related to another branch of the family there had been some feud in his father's time, and he had known little or nothing of her. He had heard vaguely that she had made a foolish marriage and had been, disowned by her parents. His first actual knowledge of her had been a letter which some people might have regarded as fulsome, but which he thought very proper, explaining that she had been left a widow in poor circumstances and begging for assistance. A personal interview had convinced him that she had the manners of a lady, that she seemed capable, and would be a grateful recipient of his bounty. He offered her a home, and within a week she had reorganised his wife's sick room and the household in general.

The marchesa had died three months later, and she had stayed on to keep house for the widower and to act as duenna to his son's young wife.

She had made herself indispensable; she fitted perfectly into the pattern of his life. This was satisfactory, but only as a basis. It was not altogether what she wanted.

To understand Amalia Marucci it was necessary to know her past, not the carefully edited and abbreviated version which she kept, so to speak, by her, but the actual facts.

At seventeen she had run away with Ettore Marucci, who had bribed a maid servant to carry notes to her. They had gone from Verona, where she lived with her parents, to Venice, where they took a small furnished flat and gave card parties. Ettore's raffish good looks and jovial manners and Amalia's beauty attracted clients, and before long they were able to move to a house on the Canale San Gregorio, with a garden and a back and side entrances on another waterway which often proved very convenient. They prospered. There was roulette upstairs and card rooms on the ground floor, and apartments where meetings could be arranged. The bored wives of elderly or neglectful husbands found Amalia an admirably discreet and sympathetic confidante. Ettore, something of a bully behind his genial façade, knew how to handle the bad losers.

There had been some bad moments. There had been two accidents that might have been suicide, and one unexplained disappearance. After a while the Casa Ferrucci acquired a rather sinister reputation, but there was never anything the police could take hold of—or so they said.

Throughout the dubious circumstances of their life together, Ettore and Amalia remained a devoted couple. Ettore was a full-blooded animal, but his lapses were never serious or very lasting. Amalia saw to that, and she was faithful to him as a tigress to her mate. They had one child, the boy Silvio, a cold, pale, subtilised version of his father, a strange child with a terrifying cold precocity that sometimes startled even his parents.

The vogue of the Casa Marucci came to an end when Ettore died of pneumonia, after three days' illness. Amalia tried to carry on, but the man she hired as manager had not the knack of dealing with their clientele. Within six months the place had closed down, and the widow was left with nothing but what she got from the sale of the furniture.

Mother and son together set themselves to wring a living from a reluctant world. Amalia, in her widow's weeds, haunted the churches, watching for the women who had been foolish enough to make her a confidante. A whispered hint or threat and money changed hands. They dared not brush her aside, for if they did she wrote letters, begging letters, humble on the surface, but with some reference to old times. She made little pincushions and other trifles and sold them to her victims for ten times what they were worth, and found an acrid satisfaction in watching them squirm, like butterflies pinned alive to a board, making feeble efforts to escape. But the sums they saved for her from their housekeeping and dress allowances were never large, and when they gave her jewellery, pretending to their husbands that they had lost it, she had to take what the old racketeer in the Merceria chose to give her for it, so that, try as she might, she remained shabby and poor.

Silvio fended for himself. He joined various youth organisations promoted by the Fascist Party, always contriving to avoid the harder and more distasteful tasks. He soon found ways of making money, and at thirteen he was known as *il biondino*, a tout for a brothel, flashing like a silver fish through the dark waters of the Venetian underworld.

At last Amalia had decided to write to the marchese Gualtieri. He might acknowledge the distant relationship, and Mont Alvino was so far away that he was not likely to have heard anything to her disadvantage. His answer had exceeded her highest hopes. The Venetian chapter of their lives was ended, and for nearly three years now the Villa had been her home, her harbour of refuge, and Silvio's headquarters.

At first she had been too glad to be free of all the hardships and ignominies of her former existence to do more than consolidate her position. After the marchesa's death she was virtually the mistress of the house. Gualtieri was old-fashioned and it seemed natural and right to him that his son's wife and her young cousin should be subject to the direction of an older woman. He was seldom at the Villa himself, for he was something of a scholar, with a taste for historical research, and he preferred to live in Rome where he had access to libraries. He was fond of his daughter-in-law, but he thought her a fool. Amedeo would have found that out if he had lived long enough, but perhaps he would not have minded, and if she had continued docile and obedient, she would have done well enough. As it was, he thought she could not come to any harm with anyone so eminently efficient and sensible as Donna Amalia to keep a sharp eye on her.

Amalia was inclined to agree that Chiara was easily managed, but she was not so sure of Alda. The girl was well-mannered, but there was a rebellious gleam at times in those hazel eyes. It was surprising, thought la Marucci, as she brushed her hair in the cool twilight of her shuttered room, how heartily she disliked the marchesina's young relative. Well, something might be done about that, and before very long.

Alda meanwhile was walking along the dusty country road to the Porta Romana with old Caterina. The cook was grumbling about la Marucci's meanness with the housekeeping money, and Alda was pretending to listen to complaints she had heard very often before. She had not slept as well as usual, and every time she woke she thought of the young Englishman lying on the straw in the Donati's cowshed, with the matted fair hair sticking out between the folds of the clumsy blood-stained bandage, and the sunken blue eyes anxious and wary as the eyes of a hunted animal.

"Caterina," she said suddenly, "do you know anything about the English?"

"I? *Sicuro*. When I was a young girl in Florence, I served an English family. They paid well, and they were kind to me. The signora was *simpaticissima*," said the old woman warmly.

Alda did not ask herself why she was pleased by this tribute to their present enemy. She said, "Why are we fighting them?"

Caterina shrugged her thin shoulders. "How should I know? It is those above. They take our men away, all the best and the strongest, all the young men—"

"All but Silvio," murmured Alda.

"That one—" said Caterina derisively. And then, in a different tone, "If I were you, signorina, I would be careful of that one. I say no more."

They had reached the town gate. The dogana official glanced into Caterina's empty market basket, treated Alda to a bold stare of admiration, and waved them on.

In the piazza they parted, Caterina to plunge happily into the chattering crowds in the market, and Alda to climb the great flight of marble steps that led to the west door of the Duomo.

A beggar lifted the leather curtain for her to pass in. She dropped a soldo in his dirty, outstretched palm and made her way to one of the side altars, where she found a chair and knelt to say a prayer.

After a while she got up and walked over to one of the row of confessionals. Several girls and women were waiting their turn near one of the others, but Alda's spiritual director was not so popular, and she was able to kneel down at once and whisper through the pierced metal screen.

Don Luigi Cappelli was a gentle old man whom nature had never intended for preferment in the church or the world. His boots had been patched again and again, and his cassock was green with age. He had few penitents and most of them were as poor and as obscure as himself. He did not know why this young girl had chosen to come to him. If he had known that it was because she felt sorry for him in his old age and his poverty he would have smiled.

When she had made her confession and listened to his brief admonitions and been absolved, she still knelt there.

"What more is there, my child?"

"Will you give me your advice—still under the seal?"

She heard him move behind the screen. There was a brief pause.

Then he said, "Yes. What is troubling you?"

She told him. "He is an enemy," she ended. "Is it wrong to try to help him?"

Another pause. Then he said, "No. But what can you do?"

"I haven't thought of a way yet. But he isn't safe there."

"I heard that an English plane passed over here during the night a week ago. It may have crashed, or this man may have been dropped by parachute. You realise, my child, that he may be a spy."

"Marietta said he was wearing an airman's overalls—at least that is what they sounded like from her description. She and her mother buried them in the wood."

"Is he well hidden?"

"He's lying in the empty cowshed, and they keep the door locked."

Don Luigi had learned through long practice to pitch his voice so that only his penitent, kneeling before the grille, could hear him. He said, "There are rumours that Germans will be stationed here. They might come any day. If they do, they will comb the countryside for provisions. They are like locusts. If they found this Englishman it would go hard with those who sheltered him."

"What shall we do?"

"Is he badly hurt?"

"I don't know. He was cut and bruised and very weak. I think perhaps he had been without food for several days."

"If he can walk I have thought of a place where I believe he would be safe. It would be a risk, but if he was found, he need not involve others. I will find out if it can be arranged. Filomena will be at the Villa to-morrow morning to fit on a new dress she is making for the signora Marucci. Look out for her. She will tell you what to do."

"How did you know—" stammered Alda.

Filomena was the little dressmaker who worked by the day mending and altering. She was clever and very cheap, and bore la Marucci's bullying meekly.

"She is my niece," said the old priest gently. "She lives with me. Go now, *figlia mia.*"

As Alda walked back to the Villa, she felt as if a weight had been lifted off her shoulders. She could not imagine what Don Luigi meant to do, but he had sounded confident. So he was Filomena's uncle. Now that she knew the connection she realised that they were alike in their physical insignificance, small, faded, even dingy-looking, with—if you gave them a second glance—a kind of simple unaffected goodness that shone through the dull envelope of flesh like the light in a horn lanthorn. Filomena, with her short-sighted eyes straining over the fine stitches, born to be overworked and put upon by employers like Donna Amalia.

Alda thought, "But why should they be involved? It's my doing—" Her heart sank as she turned in at the gates of the Villa.

"He is better," said Marietta cheerfully, as she unlocked the door of the cowshed. "This morning he asked for warm water to wash himself. That shows, la mamma says, that he is a real Englishman. Warm water. They are always asking for it."

He was sitting up, blinking at the light, and Alda saw at once that the bearded face was less haggard and even younger than she had thought.

He said, "Sorry I can't get up. At least I could, but I might fall down again. I'm still rather wonky."

"You are very nice and polite," said Alda smiling. She sat down on the stool Marietta had brought in for her.

"I hoped you'd come again," he said. "I can speak a few words of Italian, but not enough. Look. This girl and her mother have been very decent to me, but is it all right? I mean, is it going to get them into trouble?"

Alda nodded. "It might. That is why I'm afraid you must be moved. I am sorry." She saw the muscles about his jaw contract as if he was preparing to make an immediate physical effort.

"O.K.," he said. "Do you want me to go now?"

"No. Not until after dark in any case. And you must remain, of course, until you are strong enough to walk. A hiding-place is ready for you, but you will have to go to it on foot through the woods."

"I'll go to-night. I can manage all right if I'm not hurried and they'll give me a stick to lean on."

"Are you sure?" she asked anxiously.

"I can manage," he repeated, with more confidence than he actually felt. "But how shall I find my way?"

"My friend, who is going to help you, is a priest. He has always lived here, and when he was a boy he found an underground room, a sort of cave, on the hillside above the town. He found it by accident and the entrance is screened by undergrowth. He used to go there sometimes to play, but he never told anyone. He has not been there for fifty years, but he is sure that if it had been discovered by anyone else there would have been talk about it. He is going there to-night and he will take some provisions." She took a piece of paper from her handbag. "This is a plan to show you the way. I am sorry it is so crumpled. His niece, Filomena, had to slip it into my hand when nobody was looking."

He took it from her and studied it.

She bent over him, tracing the lines with her forefinger. "This is where you are now. This dot. If you went due west, down the hill, the way I shall be going in a few minutes, you would come to the Villa Gualtieri where I live. The Villa is about half a mile outside the town, on the main road going south. What you have to do is to go north from here through the woods. Don't go either up or downhill. After a while you will come to a small clearing and can look down on the town. There will be a path there, but you must not follow it. Go straight on. Don Luigi will be there looking out for you. Is that clear?"

"I think so. Thanks. I can't thank you enough. By the way my name's Drew, Richard Drew. May I know yours?"

"I am Alda Olivieri." She turned to the peasant girl, who had been standing by, patiently waiting to be enlightened. "He will go to-night. Marietta, as soon as it is dark. See that he has some food before he starts. The clothes he is wearing now belong to your husband?"

"Si, signorina."

Richard intervened. "Look here. I'd like to make it up to them for their kindness, but my pocket-book with my money and papers has gone. I crawled a longish way, you know, and I fancy I was delirious. I may have chucked it away. Will you ask her to take this? I'd like her to have it." He pulled a signet ring off his finger and offered it to Mari-etta, who shook her head and backed away.

Alda jumped up and went outside with her. Richard, waiting, heard the murmur of their voices. Alda came back presently, alone.

"She won't take it. She says it is too much. If you had had some money she might have accepted a few lire for the shirt and trousers. It is a pity your pocket-book is lost, but it can't be helped. Unfortunately," she added simply, "I have no money either. I have to ask for every soldo and explain how I am going to spend it. I must go now." She stood, looking down at him. "Good luck," she said.

"Shan't I be seeing you again?" he asked anxiously.

"I don't know. Perhaps."

She hesitated a moment, as if there was something else she wanted to say, and then she went out. The door was closed and he heard the key turned in the lock. He leaned forward, grimacing with the pain of his strained and bruised muscles, and began to rub his legs and feet! Somehow, by hook or by crook, he must be in trim to walk again within a few hours. He wondered what had happened to the rest of the crew. Pellico, who was to have been dropped here-abouts, had just baled out when the engine trouble started. After that it was difficult to remember. The sickening jerk as the parachute opened, a red light in the sky before he lost consciousness. The plane must have crashed the other side of the mountains. A week ago. More. They must have been posted missing. Hard lines on Lindsay, who got married during his last leave. Just as well, thought Richard, that he had no close ties. His married sister at Hampstead would be sorry.

Yes, poor old Chloe would cry when the wire came from the War Office. But in her heart she would be saying, "Thank God it isn't John."

Alda. Were those what they called hazel eyes? Green with golden brown lights in them.

He lay down again wearily, sweating in the airless gloom. He was itching all over. He had seen the fleas when the door was open, hopping about on the dusty brick floor.

After a while he slept. Night had fallen when Marietta came in with a lamp and a bowl of bean stew. When he had eaten it she gave him an old patched blue cloth cape and a hunk of black bread. He struggled to his feet and reached the door and there she handed him a stick of olive wood with a solid crook handle that fitted well into the palm of his hand.

"That is the way—" she pointed, a dim figure in the faint star light. She had extinguished her lamp. In the room above the child was whimpering, and the old woman was crooning a lullaby.

Richard said, "Thank you again. God bless you," and limped away, a shadow crossing the clearing and soon lost to sight under the trees.

The going was not easy. He ached from head to foot and was shaking with weakness and a touch of fever. After a time it was an effort of will to put one foot before the other, and he leaned more and more heavily on his stick and stumbled more often and was slower getting up again.

At last, after what seemed hours of agonising strain, something moved near him and a quiet voice said, "You have arrived. Give me your hand—"

He said hoarsely, "I couldn't have gone much farther." The hand that gripped his had the cold dry texture of old age, but it had also a comforting firmness.

"On your knees, *figlio mio*. Not to pray," said the voice, with a little laugh, "but to crawl through this undergrowth."

When they were in the cave, his guide readjusted the sacks that screened the hole by which they had entered, struck a match and lit one wick of a brass lucerna standing on the ground. Richard saw that his new friend was a small grey-haired priest in a very shabby cassock. Beyond him, as the light flickered, the shadows of two persons semi-recumbent on a bed were thrown on a wall. It was as if they had been sleeping and had started up in surprise at an intrusion.

Richard gaped. "Good Lord! It's an Etruscan burial chamber."

Don Luigi, who knew no English, understood quite enough. He waved a proprietary hand, beaming with satisfaction. "I discovered it. I kept it to myself. I used to come here to play. No, I was not afraid. They have kind faces. I called them auntie and uncle. I gave them no cause to be angry. I did not meddle with their plates and cups of red and black ware. I did not rob her of her gold necklace and her brooch and earrings. I trust you to respect them as your hosts."

"O.K.," muttered Richard. He sat down with a groan on the blanket Don Luigi had spread for him and unlaced his shoes. Later he was to realise that Don Luigi's accidental discovery of an Etruscan tomb was the only, but never failing source of pride, the only splash of colour in that subfusc existence, and to make amends for his present indifference. Just then he was too tired to care. Don Luigi looked for a moment like a child that had been disappointed of a treat, and then, recovering himself, displayed the contents of the unwieldy parcel he had brought with him from the town.

There was a loaf of bread, a piece of cheese, some dried apricots, a small bottle of olive oil, a cup and plate of thick brown ware and a knife and spoon. There was also a battered tin saucepan full of water.

"I brought it from the stream," explained Don Luigi. "You will have to fetch it for yourself. It is quite near. You can't miss it. If you go during the night you are not likely to meet anyone. The only people passing this way live in the podere a mile farther on. Pietro Lippi and his mother and his younger brother, who is deaf and dumb, *poveaccio*. I sometimes visit them, and that will be useful now. There is food enough here to last you two days, or perhaps three if you are careful. I will come again as soon as I can. *Felice notte, figlio mio*. Sleep well."

The dazed blue eyes were raised to his with a trustfulness that the old priest found touching. "You're a real good Samaritan, sir. It's too kind—"

"*Per niente*. There," Don Luigi bent over him, his hands gentle as a woman's. "This dry fern will serve for a pillow. If you should hear movements and voices outside, keep still. But it isn't likely. I am leaving you a box of matches, but don't keep the lamp burning if you think there is anyone about."

He extinguished the lamp and left Richard in the dark.

When Don Luigi came again two days later, it was in the middle of the afternoon. Richard welcomed him warmly.

Though the knee he had strained when coming to earth still pained him, he was much more himself. His temperature had gone down to normal. He had found the stream and though it was only a trickle oi water running downhill between stones, he had contrived to wash in it, and later, when he returned to his hiding-place, he had shaved off the seven days' growth of stubble. The priest gave him a parcel of food before he fished a crumpled envelope out of a pocket of his dingy cassock.

"A letter for you from Signorina Alda. You were not expecting to see her, naturally. It would not be proper. It would be dangerous."

"Yes. Yes, of course," said Richard, trying not to sound disappointed.

"I will leave you to read your letter," said Don Luigi "and you can write an answer if you wish. I will see that she gets it. I am going on now to that podere I told you of. The younger son, the deaf and dumb one, is ill. I will come here again on my way back, in perhaps two hours' time."

He wiped his hot face with a bandana handkerchief and set off again.

Left to himself, Richard replaced the screen of sack over the entrance. A little daylight filtered into the underground chamber through a crack in the roof at one corner but it was not bright enough to read by, and he lit the lamp. He had been hoping for a visit from Alda. He had never thought of a letter. He opened and read it eagerly. He was not a very susceptible young man, but Alda's long-lashed hazel eyes had made a considerable impression, and since he last saw her, the slight figure in the pink silk frock had flitted in and out of his dreams.

She had written in English, in a fine flowing Italian hand, and with the violet ink most in use in Latin countries.

"Dear Mr. Drew,

"Don Luigi and his niece, who sometimes works at our house, hope to keep you supplied with food, and he thinks you will be quite safe in your present hiding-place for the present. When you are quite well and strong again we must think what can be done. I am afraid you will be very dull nearly always in the dark, as Don Luigi will not be able to let you have much oil for your lamp. You must try to sleep as much as possible. It will help to pass the time. I am sorry I cannot come to see you. Don Luigi says it would be very unwise, and I am afraid he is right. At the podere it was easy. I go there two or three times a week to see my cousin's baby. Marietta, as I suppose you realised, is her foster-mother. My cousin is delicate and cannot climb the hill herself, so I go instead, to make sure that the child is thriving. If there had been light enough for you to read I could have lent you some books. *I Promessi Sposi* for instance. It is a pity. I do not like to think of you sitting alone in the dark, but you must be patient.

"With salutations and best wishes.

"Yours sincerely,

"ALDA OLIVIERI."

Richard never had any difficulty in expressing himself on paper. Don Luigi had supplied him with a cheap writing-pad. He wrote industriously, covering page after page with his small firm script. Her shy formal style pleased him, but he did not try to emulate it. His letter was a spontaneous outpouring. He wrote, though he was hardly himself aware of it, as a man writes to the woman who has filled his mind.

"I expect the old gentleman is right. I don't want you to take any risks. We shall meet again later on. I'll see to that. Meanwhile, I am seeing you with my mind's eye in that pink sleeveless thing you wore and the hat with the brim that shades your face. I want to know all about you, and I am going to pump His Reverence. I hope you won't mind. And I want to tell you about myself. Before the war I worked in a bank, and, in my spare time, I wrote essays and articles and short stories and posted them to editors, and sometimes they appeared in print and sometimes they didn't. I was at Oxford, Worcester College, and only a pass degree I'm sorry to say. I spent two long vacations, '36 and '37, in Italy, and that's when I picked up my Italian, such as it is. It's very sweet of you to think of lending me books, but I can pass my time here very pleasantly thinking of you. And I shan't be here long. I have to get on with my job. You won't, of course, think of me as an enemy. It was always ridiculous that your country and mine should be opposed, and it would never have happened if it had not been for that ghastly twerp with the prognathous jaw. You know who I mean? I give you three guesses. Please go on being kind and write to me again. Not Mr. Drew. Just Richard, or, if you prefer it, Dick. And let it be soon because, as I said before, I shall have to move on as soon as I am fit.

"Meanwhile believe me, your very humble and devoted servant,

RICHARD DREW."

Don Luigi, when he arrived, accepted the letter without comment.

Richard asked him if he had any news of the war. "We hear of victories. Always victories," said the old priest. "No one believes the newspapers, or the wireless."

"Don't you hear the B.B.C.?"

"I have never had a radio. They cost money. And reception is bad in Mont Alvino because of the hills all round. But there are rumours that the English and Americans may try to land in Italy, if they have not already done so. There are many trains going south, and some say they are full of Germans."

"I see," said Richard. He hesitated. "The line is clear? There hasn't been any—any interruptions?"

"I have not heard of any." Don Luigi cleared his throat. "They are saying that Germans may be stationed in Mont Alvino," he said unhappily.

Richard grinned. "Your dear allies."

"Italy has been misled and betrayed, *figlio mio*," said the priest gently.

Though there was no shade of reproof in his voice, Richard felt abashed and mumbled, "I beg your pardon."

"I must be going," began Don Luigi.

"Stay a little longer," urged Richard. "Tell me, has the Signorina Alda a father or brothers fighting?"

"Neither. She was an only child and she has lost both parents. She is related to the daughter-in-law of the marchese Gualtieri. The two young girls were brought up together, but the marchesina was an heiress, and her cousin, *poverina,* has nothing. The marchese has given her a home. His daughter-in-law is glad of her company, especially now that she has lost her husband. There is an older woman, also a widow, and a distant relative of the marchese. She is a very capable person and the young marchesina leaves everything to her. Gualtieri himself is often away from home."

All this did not convey very much to Richard. He said, "Are the Gualtieri well known locally?"

His Italian was stiff but he managed to frame the question that had been in his mind.

Don Luigi smiled. "The Gualtieri have lived in the Villa since the middle of the seventeenth century, when it was built. Before that they had a palace in the Via Larga. It is still there, but is let to various tenants. There has never been a Gualtieri Pope, but three times since the Cinquecento Gualtieri have been elected to the Sacred College of Cardinals. They have come down in the world. No longer powerful or wealthy, the family seems to be dwindling away, dying out in the shadow of past glories. The marchese was an only child. He had one son, and he was posted missing three months ago. They say the marchese has not been seen to smile since."

"Do you know him?"

"I? I have known him by sight ever since I can remember. As a young man riding a chestnut horse, driving in his wife's carriage on Thursday evenings when there was music in our public gardens. Later in the automobile with his son driving. The marchesa never left the grounds of the Villa then, she was an invalid for some years, though in the end her death was sudden and unexpected to many people. The marchesa was very devout, very charitable to the poor, but

I was not her confessor. I am a very obscure person, Signor Drew. I am never likely to cross the threshold of the Villa. My niece goes there every day just now, but that is because she has been engaged to sew for the Signora Marucci. It is she who will see that the Signorina Alda gets your letter."

"I suppose Alda does not meet many—many people in the ordinary way?" said Richard.

Don Luigi shook his head. "A signorina, *per bene*, brought up as she has been, should be carefully guarded and cherished until a suitable husband is found for her. But she has no dowry. The marchesina loves her, but she is young and thoughtless, and only considers her as a companion for herself. In that household she is unregarded, of less account than a pet dog or kitten. But she is a good child. She has a better head than the marchesina. A good child. But you have seen for yourself—"

CHAPTER IV
THE TANGLED WEB

THE work to be done had accumulated. There were new summer dresses to be made for Donna Amalia, for the marchesina, and even, if time allowed, for Alda Olivieri. That, however, was not certain. Donna Amalia had retained the services of the dressmaker for a fortnight, beating her down, incidentally, to a lower figure than she usually obtained for her services.

"You must remember, Filomena, that you have your meals here, and if you work well you will have the marchesina's recommendation. That is worth something."

Filomena had to agree. Times were hard, but la Marucci, she reflected, was even harder. She agreed with the servants in disliking the handsome, middle-aged woman whom the marchese had left in charge of his household.

Not a minute of her time and not a needleful of thread must be wasted or Donna Amalia, her black eyes snapping, would know the reason why. The town clocks were striking nine as Filomena trudged up the dusty avenue in the thin lacy shade of the acacias.

Chiara and her cousin had established themselves in the garden, in the shade of a hedge of clipped ilex. Chiara was lying on a wicker chaise longue, and Alda was perched on the rim of the lily pool, throwing crumbs to the goldfish who swam up, open mouthed, from under the flat green floating leaves.

Chiara was looking pale but very lovely, her golden hair loose over the silk cushions. "There's Filomena," she said languidly, as the drab little figure appeared round the corner of the house.

"She's carrying a parcel. It may be the stuff you chose. I'll go and meet her," said Alda quickly.

Chiara smiled faintly at this unnecessary display of energy. It was so like Alda to run about and make herself hot.

The little dressmaker turned off the path on to the grass as she saw Alda coming towards her.

"Buon giorno, signorina."

"Same to you, Filomena. Have you anything for me? Here, take this."

The exchange of letters had been made unseen by Chiara a hundred yards away under the trees, and unseen also from the house, and they both breathed more freely. Filomena said, "I managed to get a dress length of the black and white flowered chiffon, the pattern the marchesina wanted. Shall I show it to her before I go into the house?"

"Yes. Let her see it. I was so glad she took some interest. It is the first time since—she used to be fond of pretty clothes." Alda's eyes filled with tears.

"Ah, *poverina*," murmured Filomena. "It's six years since mine died of wounds in Abyssinia."

Alda glanced towards the house. "Can you stay now? Won't she be angry?"

"E vero," the little dressmaker said anxiously. "She will be waiting. I must go. Listen, signorina. Silvio Marucci is back. I saw him just now on the steps of the Municipio with two German officers."

That was bad news. Alda disliked Silvio, and she was also afraid of him. She did not know why. He consistently ignored her. She did not mind that. There was something more. "He makes my flesh creep," she had told Chiara, but Chiara only laughed and said he was quite good-looking, spoilt, of course, by his mother, and very vain. Amedeo had loathed him, but would not say why.

She said, "He'll be coming on here then. Germans? Are you sure?"

"Certain. Those thick red necks, and little eyes like stones. Besides, they wore German uniforms."

Alda said: "Give me the parcel. I will show the material to the marchesina. Filomena—tell him to be careful. Warn him—"

She went back to Chiara and they spent the rest of the morning as usual, idly turning over the leaves of fashion books, discussing styles and patterns, lounging in the shade. Chiara asked what Filomena had been saying. "She told me she saw Silvio in the town."

Chiara yawned. "He'll be here for lunch then probably." She frowned. "He makes himself at home. Since—since—he couldn't really take Amedeo's place, could he, Alda?"

"Of course not. He's only a distant relation. He has no right here. The marchese could always send him away if he—if he presumed—"

"He is very clever," murmured Chiara, "and so is she. But perhaps we may find a way."

Alda looked at her curiously. "What do you mean?"

"Wait and see," said Chiara teasingly. "I can have my secrets, as well as you."

Alda's face was burning. She loved Chiara but she never told her anything. It had been the same at the convent. She meant no harm, but she could not be trusted not to talk at the wrong moment and to the wrong people. Chiara might be empty-headed, but she could be disconcertingly shrewd at unexpected moments, and this was one of them.

She smiled, and putting out a thin finger, gently touched the. younger girl's flushed cheek.

"Don't look so frightened, *cara mia*. I shall not give you away to la Marucci. In any case I know nothing. There is somebody—but I cannot imagine who it can be. We have no visitors, we see no one. Never mind. I shall be patient, and one day you will tell me all about it. Meanwhile, *zitta!*" She laid the same finger on her own lips.

From where they sat, they could not see the avenue, but they heard a car arrive and stop with a screaming of gears that sounded like Silvio, who sawed at machinery as he sawed at a horse's mouth. When they went into the dining-room for lunch he was there with his mother. His thick fair hair was like a primrose satin cap on his narrow head. He looked very slick and dapper in his smartly cut black Fascist shirt and breeches and black riding boots. He greeted the two girls with unsmiling formality, giving first the Fascist salute, and then bowing stiffly from the waist to kiss the marchesina's hand.

During the meal he talked exclusively to his mother, who listened complacently. Things were moving, he said, allied attempts to land on Italian soil were doomed. The *cani Inglesi* and the *Americani* would be flung back into the sea to drown like blind puppies.

"The English dogs," he repeated, with angry satisfaction. "My friend the Baron von Reuterhausen was saying so this morning. I would have asked him to lunch but I was afraid there would not be anything fit to eat."

Donna Amalia sighed and said that catering was increasingly difficult. She sent Caterina every day to the market, but she was an old fool, and there was no meat or fish or white flour, and very little oil.

Chiara had opened her mouth to speak, but thought better of it. She was too timid to venture on a frontal attack. Alda, too, was silent, though there were several things she longed to say. Pietro was shuffling round the table, changing the plates, his gnarled hands in their carefully washed and mended white cotton gloves, were shaking perceptibly.

The dessert was a dish of wild strawberries drenched in red wine. Silvio took a large helping.

"I wish they would choke him," thought Alda, as she got up to follow Chiara from the room, after dropping an almost invisible curtsey to Donna Amalia.

"The insolence," said Chiara, as they went upstairs. "'I wanted to say it is not your house, but I'm such a coward. I can't bear scenes. They make me ill. The marchese does not like Germans. He would never invite them here. It is intolerable. If only his eyes could be opened."

"I can't see how," said Alda. "He has such confidence in her. She flatters him, and Silvio effaces himself, when the marchese is home."

"Wait," said Chiara, "wait." And then fretfully, "my head aches. It's the worry—"

Alda left her lying on her bed in a darkened room. She was going up the hill presently to see how the baby was getting on, but first she would shut herself in her room to read Richard's letter and at least begin to answer it. She had been carrying it about all this time in her pochette with her handkerchief and compact, and lipstick. She had been acutely conscious of it as it lay on her knees during lunch. If Silvio knew—

Alda read her letter quickly the first time, to get a general idea of what Richard had to say, and then more slowly, puzzling over some phrases. The English she had learned from the nuns had not included such expressions as fed up, browned off, wizard or okay, but the gist of it all seemed to be that he was quite well again and that he only remained in his present hiding-place under protest because Friar Laurence was in such a blue funk at the very thought when he suggested getting a move on.

"A blue funk?" thought Alda, and wished she had an English-Italian dictionary in her room.

She sat down to write two pages of exhortation and advice.

> "You must listen to what he says—I do not mention names in case this should fall into the wrong hands— but I cannot imagine why you call him Friar Laurence.

You must be patient. Remember that any imprudence may involve others as well as yourself. I know it must be very dull for you, and I am afraid you do not really get enough to eat. I wish I could come and see you, but I am afraid I might be followed, or questions might be asked which I should find it difficult to answer. I can tell lies if necessary, but I am not good at it. I enclose a little snapshot of myself since you ask for it. It was taken in the garden here last summer by my cousin's husband. I think I look very funny. It was perhaps out of focus. He and Chiara and I were laughing. Poor boy, he was so nice, so *simpatico*, and so young to die. When will this war end? I pray for that every day. I must stop now. I say again patience."—Alda underlined the word three times. "I think of you very often, and remain your sincere friend. A."

On her way out she passed through the landing, where Filomena, her flat chest bristling with pins, was tacking the lining of the silk coat she was turning for Donna Amalia.

"The signorina is going out in all this heat?"

"Only to see the *bambino*."

Alda glanced about her. All the doors opening on the landing were closed. At this hour la Marucci should be resting on her bed, though Alda knew they were never really safe from her poking and prying. The letters changed hands, and Alda, her spirits rising at the prospect of getting away from the Villa even for an hour or two, ran down the stairs.

Silvio's car was drawn up outside the door. It occurred to Alda to wonder how he had paid for it and how he got petrol when petrol was so scarce.

Silvio lounged against the balustrade smoking a cigarette. He was looking at her, his heavy-lidded blue eyes narrowed against the light, with his insolent half smile.

"Do you want to go for a drive?"

"No, thank you."

"On foot, in this heat?"

Alda, to her own annoyance, felt obliged to explain. "I am only going up to the podere, where Chiara's baby is at nurse."

"To be sure," he said, still on a note of raillery, "the son and heir. Is he very sickly?"

"Not at all," she said angrily, "he's a very fine child."

"Davvero?" he said, with a drawl that conveyed complete disbelief.

Alda realised that he was trying to make her lose her temper. Looking at his pale sneering face, she thought she saw how he would enjoy hurting her if he could. Why? She had never done him any harm. But he probably knew that she and Chiara regarded him and his mother as interlopers at the Villa. She brushed by him without answering, and until she had turned the corner of the house and was out of sight she was uneasily aware that he followed her with his eyes.

Donna Amalia was sitting before her mirror when Silvio came into her room. She did not turn her head, but watched his reflection as he came up behind her.

"Admiring yourself, *mamma mia*?"

She replied with an expressive grimace. "Not exactly. Fifteen, even ten years ago I should have no doubts. Now—there is still something left."

Silvio lit another cigarette. "The marchese," he said, "is a creature of habit. He has his old-fashioned code of honour. That must be respected. He admires and esteems you, and such admirable sentiments are an excellent foundation for a second marriage. But at present he is in no need of a wife, since he is perfectly satisfied with the mistress whom he has been keeping in Rome ever since the late marchesa's health failed."

"You have found out more about her?"

"I have. Her name is Rosina Bianchi. She is not in the least glamorous, but she is comfortably plump, an animated cushion, cheerful and good-tempered, and has no extravagant tastes. She has, in fact, all the bourgeois virtues and is entirely faithful to her elderly admirer. While he has her your case is hopeless. If he lost her he might turn to you for consolation."

"Where does she live? Do you know that?"

"Yes. She has a small flat in the Ludovisi quarter."

"His daughter-in-law will prevent it if she can. She hates me."

"What can she do? She's afraid of you. The other girl is more dangerous."

"Why do you say that?"

"The way she looked at me just now. I wouldn't trust that little bitch very far if I were you. She seems to come and go just as she likes."

"She is of no importance. She can only hope to find a husband if the marchese provides a dowry, and why should he do that? I leave her alone. If she makes a slip, as she may, it will give me a handle if I want to get rid of her."

"You mean if she picks up a lover?"

"Precisely. It may happen any time, if it hasn't already. The fruit is ripe," said la Marucci cynically, "ready to fall into somebody's hand. Girls of that age. Perhaps one of your German friends? But he would have to take a little trouble. The child was well brought up, she has standards of conduct."

"Then they would have no use for her," smiled Silvio. "They have no time to waste on bows and compliments. I must be going. I am driving them back to Rome this evening, but I shall be returning in a few days. Think over what I have told you and let me know if you want action. *Addio, mammina.*"

For some time after he had left her she sat frowning, lost in thought.

CHAPTER V

RICHARD MARKS TIME

DON Luigi came to Richard's hiding-place as often as he could, but sometimes two or three days elapsed between his visits. He could not make too marked a change in his habits without attracting attention. In an Italian working-class quarter the women are always at their doors, knitting, plaiting straw, making pillow lace, combing their children's heads, or merely idling, and everyone knew the old priest and his widowed niece who went out to ladies' houses to sew. Already there had been comments.

"You're always bringing home parcels nowadays, Filomena."

"Kitchen scraps. My clients are very kind—"

Food was a problem, for so many things were rationed. It was as well for Richard's peace of mind that he never guessed how often they denied themselves a second slice of bread or a scrap more cheese so that he might have enough to eat.

During the day there was just light enough in that rock-hewn grave to see the two semi-recumbent figures of its rightful occupants. Richard tried not to let their sightless stare get on his nerves. He had heard vaguely of the Etruscans as a lost race that had lived in Italy before the Romans and had vanished no one quite knew how or why. He had looked at the jars of red and black pottery that had once held wheat and wine and oil, at the bone hairpins and combs, the gold fibulae and the string of blue beads, but the woman who had worn them had been dead too long, he could not bridge the gulf of three thousand years.

He worried over Pellico, who had been dropped by parachute according to plan, just before the engine began to play up. Pellico was an Italian who had lived all his life in England and was naturalised, or perhaps he was British-born. His father had owned a little restaurant in Soho, and the whole family had been wiped out by a German bomb. Young Aristide, known to his friends in the Air Force as Arry, was the only survivor. He had been dropped just outside Mont Alvino to do a job, and so far he had not done it. The crew had thought it would be a piece of cake for Arry. He would, of course, have no difficulty in passing as a native, he was dressed in Italian clothes, and supplied with Italian money and all that was necessary. Why wasn't he getting on with it? "I ought to try to make contact with him," thought Richard. Perhaps not. Pellico would probably be safer without him. He must know that the plane had crashed and might have assumed there were no survivors. "I wouldn't tag after him and cramp his style," thought Richard, "but if we could only meet once and talk things over."

Perhaps the most sensible thing would be to remain in hiding until the war was over or Italy, at any rate, had been cleared of the enemy. No. He couldn't do that. It would be putting an unbearable strain on the resources of Don Luigi and his niece. They were risking their lives for him. It couldn't go on. There was Alda, too. He thought a great deal about Alda. He wrote her long letters and he read and re-read her letters to him before burning them in the dim flame of the *lucerna*.

He relived the very few minutes they had been together in the rather malodorous cowshed at the podere, he thought of her eyes, candid and kind in the shadow of the big straw hat, of her clear young voice uttering the precise and careful English learned from the nuns. He knew a great deal more about her now than he had then, partly from her letters, and partly from Don Luigi. He knew that she was a poor relation, an unpaid dependent, her present obscure, her future uncertain, the youngest and the most defenceless member of an ill-assorted household.

"I'll get her out of all that," he thought, "some day."

At his request, Don Luigi brought him a tattered old guide to Mont Alvino, with a road map, which he managed to pick up for a few soldi on a junk stall in the market, and a map of the district giving not only the roads, but the foot-paths, published for cyclists, walkers and climbers by one of the youth organisations emulating German Strength through Joy in the comparatively easy-going days before the war. He made an intensive study of these, poring over them in the dim light that came through the crack in the roof. After a while he had the layout of the streets and their names by heart, and had as good a working knowledge of the country in a twenty-mile radius as anyone can have to get from map reading. Before long such knowledge might be extremely useful to him.

At night, he waited for the darkest hour, to creep out of his hole in the ground, wash himself in the trickling stream and refill his water jug. He was always more or less hungry, but that could not be helped, and he always tried to reassure the old priest when he apologised for bringing him so little food. Once he had a treat, two green artichokes fried in thick yellow batter, and wrapped in greasy newspaper. Don Luigi was so proud of this delicacy that Richard felt obliged to eat the nauseous concoction with a show of enthusiasm and a smacking of lips, but he was so famished that it went down more easily than he had expected. Afterwards he tried to spell out the news in the paper, but the grease had made it illegible. Don Luigi could never bring him a paper, because his copy, when he had read it, was passed on to a neighbour.

"You would be no wiser, *figlio mio*," he said. "They are full of lies. Only one thing is certain, and that is that the Germans are sending reinforcements to the south. To all intents and purposes they have occupied our country. They favour the hundred per cent Fascists like young Marucci, there is oil and butter and wine for them, and petrol for their cars, but the rest of the people are the dirt under their feet."

The German regiment that was to be stationed in Mont Alvino had not yet arrived, but they were expected any day.

"The people have been warned," said Don Luigi, "to be very careful not to create incidents. One drunken Bavarian who has got a knife in his ribs in a wine shop brawl may mean the taking of ten or twenty hostages to be sent to forced labour in Germany. That is what we have come to, signore, we who in the days of Augustus Caesar, were masters of the world."

Richard, listening to him, found himself wondering uneasily what would happen if Pellico carried out his assignment. He was taking his time over it, but perhaps something had happened to hold him up. He had instructions which had not been transmitted to the crew of the plane in which he was, for that night, a passenger. They knew what he hoped to do, but not how he was supposed to set about it, or if he could expect any help from the underground movement which certainly existed, though after twenty years of Fascism it was far less widespread and powerful than the French organisation.

The days crawled by. He wondered if he was being bleached white, like the creatures that live under a stone. He often told the old priest that he must go, but Don Luigi bogged him to stay. "A little longer, *figlio mio. Pazienza. Pazienza.*"

Chapter VI
WHAT CHIARA KNEW

FILOMENA had turned a silk coat and made two new dresses for Donna Amalia, and two black and white muslin frocks for Chiara to wear during the scorching heat of August, when her heavy widow's mourning would be unbearably heavy; she had made nothing for Alda, who had no money and wore her cousin's cast offs. Her work at the Villa was done and she had gone on to other clients. The sewing machine and the table on which she cut out her patterns had been removed from the landing.

Alda would have missed her in any case. Shut in as they were, anyone coming from the world outside was welcome. But Filomena's departure meant the interruption of her correspondence with Richard. Henceforth they could only exchange letters once a week, when she went to confession, unless she could find some good excuse to go into the town at some other time. And even that would be no use, for though she knew where Don Luigi and his niece lived, she realised that it would look very odd if she went to their flat, and that if they were both out she would not dare to leave her letter in their letter box. Her visit would be noticed by the neighbours and commented on. They would know who she was, a relation of the marchesina Gualtieri. One thing led to another.

In future she would only hear from him once a week. And so much could happen in seven days. She remembered that when Marietta had shown her the fugitive lying in the cowshed at the podere and asked her advice she had thought that to help him would be an exciting adventure.

She had known grief in her short life, she had grieved when her parents died, when Amedeo Gualtieri, who had always been kind to her, had been lost with his plane, but this ache and this longing were new. And she must keep it to herself. She must not let la Marucci see that anything was amiss.

Chiara came down the steps from the terrace to where she sat on the stone bench by the lily pool. Something seemed to have roused her from her habitual languor. Her eyes were bright and there was more colour than usual in her cheeks.

"I've been looking for you everywhere, Alda. I have something to tell you. It's good news. I give you three guesses."

"Something about the war?"

"*Per carita!* What do I care about that—now. Something nearer, more important to us."

Alda shook her head. "I can't imagine. You'll have to tell me."

"My dear, aren't we always saying we should be happy enough here if it weren't for you know who? But so long as the marchese thinks her indispensable, there isn't a chance. But Amedeo sometimes wondered if she had always been such a pattern of all the virtues. And the other day I thought of something. She and her precious Silvio came here from Venice, and I remembered that nice young Venetian couple we met in Como when we were on our honeymoon. They were Venetians. We exchanged cards, but we never wrote or heard from them.

"But I looked through the odds and ends, picture postcards and dried flowers and so on, that I have always kept in memory of the happiest days of my life, and I found her card. So I wrote to her and asked her if she knew anything about a certain person, and, because I am certain that she reads all my letters, I asked her to reply undercover to Caterina. I warned Caterina, of course, that a letter intended for me might arrive. She was quite willing. I gave her a little present."

"You planned all this without saying a word to me."

Chiara giggled. "I wanted to show you that you're not the only one who can keep a secret. Yes, I know you have one, though I don't know what it is."

"Nonsense!" Alda looked at her cousin with affectionate exasperation. This was almost the Chiara of the old convent school days, gay, mischievous, irresponsible, whom the old French nun. Mother Angelique, called *tête de serin*. "Never mind me," she urged. "Go on. You have heard from your Venetian friend?"

"A letter came this morning. The *postino* came into the kitchen to give it to Caterina. He couldn't make it out because he knows, of course, that she can't read. However, she told him to mind his own business, and she's been carrying it about in her apron pocket all day, until she got a chance to give it to me."

"Is it—I mean—"

"My dear, she asked her husband, and he knew. If it's the same woman, and he thinks from my description that it must be, she and her husband were definitely *mala gente*, of the underworld. They kept a gaming house. There were two mysterious disappearances which were almost, but not quite, traced to their establishment. After his death the place had to be given up, and she took to haunting the churches, dressed in shabby mourning and cadging from former clients who were afraid to say no, in case she made mischief. The boy, they say, was known to be a little monster of vice—"

"Per carita!" gasped Alda. "Is all that in the letter?"

"It is. And when the marchese comes I shall show it to him, and then we shall see," said Chiara triumphantly.

But Alda, instead of reflecting the elder girl's satisfaction, was looking white and worried.

"You have hidden the letter in a safe place?"

"Naturally. Alda, haven't you understood? Aren't you glad? He'll send her packing. He'll have no choice."

"It may not be so easy," said Alda. "You forget that Silvio is in favour with the Party. I believe he could make trouble for the marchese if he chose."

"Amedeo always said his father took no part in politics. He has kept out of things. He has given them no cause—"

"I hope you are right," said Alda, She glanced quickly over her shoulder. "What was that?"

"I didn't hear anything."

"It sounded like leaves rustling—but there isn't a breath of air to move them. Chiara, could there have been somebody on the other side of the ilex hedge?"

"In the vineyard? Not likely at this hour."

"I don't know. I don't like it."

Alda jumped up and ran along the pleached walk in the shadow of the long hedge of closely clipped ilex, until she came to an opening. She looked about and could see nobody moving among the rows of vines. But there would have been time, she thought, for an eavesdropper to get away.

That letter. Where could Chiara hide it? No place was safe from la Marucci's prying. Chiara was careless, she never locked anything up, all her possessions were left lying about. To think of her with that letter in her possession was like watching a child playing with a stick of dynamite.

"Was there anybody?"

"I don't know. I hope not. Where is it, Chiara? Have you got it with you?"

Chiara patted the black satin bag, embroidered in silver thread, that swung from her wrist. "In this!" she said gaily, "with my lipstick and my handkerchief and my fan? No, my dear. I'm not going to tell you where it is. I have put it away and it will stay where it is until the time comes to show to the marchese. You have disappointed me, Alda," she added petulantly. "I thought you would be as delighted as I am about this."

"I'm sorry," Alda said. "But I'm frightened. Those two are dangerous."

But when they went into the house for supper, everything seemed just as usual. In fact Donna Amalia seemed to be in one of her better moods and encouraged Chiara to think that the baby might be weaned in the autumn and brought back to the Villa. "You'd like that, wouldn't you, my dear? I know you are longing to have the child with you."

After supper all three sat out on the terrace, watching the fireflies sparkling in the rose bushes and the stars coming out, as the greenish pallor of the western horizon darkened to the zenith.

Alda watched Donna Amalia with renewed and rather furtive interest. She was painfully thin, but an artist would have admired the bony structure of the skull, the fine lines of neck and shoulder, the long narrow hands and feet, the feline grace and swiftness of her movements when she stooped to retrieve the cigarette holder she had dropped. She lay back in her chair, her piled-up curls blue-black against the red silk of the cushions, her magnificent black eyes half closed, and smoked placidly, ignoring the two girls who sat a little behind her in the shadow.

After a while she turned her head. The church clocks in the town were striking the hour.

"'Eleven," she said sharply, "time you were in bed, both of you. Run, along."

The habit of obedience was strong in both the girls, ingrained during their years at the convent. It would not have occurred to them to dispute the order. They rose at once murmuring *"Buona notte,"* and went into the house together.

The following days passed uneventfully at the Villa. Not far away, men sweated and fought and died, roofs and walls crashed, burying women and children in the rubble, black smoke drifted over the ruins, the tide of destruction flowed on; but no papers were delivered at the Villa, and though Silvio wrote to his mother, he made hardly any reference to the progress of the war.

Alda was looking forward to Friday, when she would go to confession and hear mass afterwards at the Duomo, and hear the latest news of Richard from Don Luigi. There would be a letter for her, and she had written one which the old priest would deliver. She started as usual with Caterina, who trudged down the dusty road towards the town gate, grumbling as she always grumbled over la Marucci's meanness. "Get this and get that. And then doles out a few lire. Salt, and *pasta* and anchovies. *Accidente—*"

Alda had been terrified that at the last minute something would happen to keep her at home. She breathed more freely, as she always did when they were out on the road. The heat and the dust did not affect her. She walked lightly, almost with a dancing step, by the side of the old woman, who was too absorbed in her grievances to notice her companion's mounting spirits, but she did peer up into her flushed and smiling face just before they parted in the piazza, and said, "*La signorina é bellina stamani.* That frock becomes you, *piccina.* Well, we are only young once." There was a knowing look on her wrinkled face as she shuffled off to the market to do her shopping. The servants at the Villa all agreed that Alda had found a lover lately, though they could not imagine who it could be. The subject was freely canvassed in the kitchen.

Alda lifted the heavy leather curtain at the church door, dipped her fingers in the nearest stoup of holy water and crossed herself before she moved forward into the incense-scented twilight of the great nave. A few women were kneeling in a side chapel where mass was being said, but otherwise the church seemed deserted. She was, perhaps, a little early. She went across to the confessional box where Don Luigi would be waiting and knelt before the grating.

"Father—"

"You have come to make your confession, *figlia mia?* I am taking the place of Don Luigi Cappelli."

"Oh—" her heart sank, down, down, like a stone. "Is he—what has happened to him?"

"He was taken ill. I understand that it was a stroke, a paralytic stroke. He is in the hospital. You must pray for him."

Alda's lips had gone dry. She had to moisten them before she could speak. "Yes. Yes, I will. When did this happen, *padre mio*?"

"It was on Monday."

Monday. Five days. What had happened meanwhile to Richard, who depended on Don Luigi for the bare necessities of life? Could Filomena take his place? Would she even know the whereabouts of his hiding place? Alda thought it unlikely.

"'I am waiting, *figlia mia*—"

The voice of the priest recalled her to her present position. She must make her confession. She pulled herself together. Faults she must try to overcome. Impatience, laziness, vanity, sins of the flesh—was it a sin to love Richard—not a word about Richard, even under the seal of the confessional. It was over at last, the tired old voice mumbling advice, prayers to be said, the absolution, and she could get up and move away, leaving another woman to take her place.

She found a chair in an empty chapel and sat down. Her knees were shaking, and she had to think what she should do next. A visit to the hospital, or should she try to see Filomena?

The dressmaker went out by the day. Would it be any use going to the flat she shared with her uncle at this hour? Alda decided that she would try the hospital first.

It was not far off, in a turning out of the piazza, a former palace of the Aldobrandinis of Mont Alvino, converted to its present uses when the municipality took it over after the death of the last survivor of the family. The long, dark, stone-paved passages echoed to the clatter of hurrying feet, the walls were white-washed, there were mingled odours of carbolic and drains. Nurses in uniform and men in white overalls, who might be doctors or students, went in and out of doors. No one paid the slightest attention to Alda. She found her way eventually into a small office where a nun was seated at a rolltop desk writing. She looked calm and efficient.

"Don Luigi Cappelli. Are you a relation?"

"No. A friend."

"This is not the hour for visitors."

"Oh, please." Alda clasped her hands appealingly. "I might not be able to come again. I am not free—it is difficult. And I want to see him. It is important—"

The nun eyed her thoughtfully. "Very well," she said finally, "I will take you to him myself. But you can only stay a few minutes. We have him in a private ward. Come with me."

The nun paused for a moment before opening the door at the end of the corridor. "He has something on his mind," she said. "I will come for you in five minutes." The room was small and clean and bare. Don Luigi was propped up with pillows in a narrow bed. At first she hardly recognised him. His face was drawn down and discoloured on one side and there was silvery white stubble on his chin. She saw relief in his eyes as they met hers. Impulsively she knelt down by the side of his bed and kissed the hand lying inert on the coverlet. She had grown very fond of Don Luigi.

"I am so sorry," she said. "You'll be better soon, I hope. You must not worry. But what about Richard? What am I to do?"

He stared at her, his dim eyes the only living thing in his distorted face. She felt rather than saw that he was making a supreme effort to answer her. He mumbled something. She leant closer, straining to catch what he was trying to say. It was no use. She could not make out one word what he was telling her, staring up at her all the while imploringly as if for reassurance? What he had to say was urgent and he believed that she followed his unintelligible murmuring. "Yes, yes," she whispered. "We shall manage, with God's help. Don't worry—"

She was glad when the nun came in to take her away. His eyes had closed, and he looked exhausted but more at peace. When they were out of the room the nun said, "Could you understand him?"

Alda shook her head. Tears were running down her face. "Not a word. But I let him think I did—"

"Good girl," said the nun approvingly. "Can you find your way out?"

Alda said she could.

The vicolo dei Scalzi was a narrow alley with a flight of steps that made it impossible for wheeled traffic. Lean cats roamed the gutters, hunting for food among the vegetable refuse, a cobbler sat at his stall patching shoes, women sat at their open windows observing the passers by or shouting remarks to neighbours across the way. Nobody in this quarter wore a hat, and Alda felt that hers made her conspicuous. The group of stout slatternly women gossiping on the doorstep of number ten stared at her when she asked if she might pass, but they were quite civil. Filomena Sartoni was at home. If the signorina would go up to the fifth floor. The door on the right.

Filomena answered the door. Her eyes were red and swollen with crying.

"Signorina Alda," she said dully. "You had better come in. Excuse the disorder." She led the way into a bare and shabby living-room. The remains of a meal had been pushed to one end of the table to make room for a sewing machine and for scattered remnants of material and crumpled paper patterns. A half-finished coat tacked together with white thread hung behind the door. The only traces of Don Luigi were a shelf of tattered books, a stoup of holy water and a garish chromolithograph of a bad modern picture of the Virgin Mary and the infant Christ in a gilt frame. On a shelf in front of the picture was a blue vase of the type that can be won as a prize on fair grounds, with a bunch of paper flowers stuffed into it.

"I have just been to the hospital," said Alda. "I had only just heard when I went to confession. I am so sorry—"

Filomena had set a chair for her, but she remained standing herself. Alda, looking up at her with eager sympathy, became aware of the rigidity of the little flat-chested figure, of something unexpectedly hard and unyielding in the sallow tear-stained face.

"It was your fault," said Filomena.

"Mine?" echoed Alda.

"It was you, wasn't it, who persuaded him to do what he need not have done, to risk prison, or a beating up, or shooting, and go without his food, and trudge for miles in the heat of the day, and wear himself out with work and worry. Not even for one of his own; for a stranger, a foreigner. And all for nothing. Not a soldo of reward. And you come and say you are sorry."

Alda gazed at her helplessly. She was taken completely by surprise. Filomena had always seemed perfectly willing to act as a go-between. Alda was too inexperienced to realise that Filomena was one of those people who, when they are hurt, hit out at random. Alda felt that the older girl was being unjust, at the same time her fundamental honesty compelled her to admit that Filomena's accusation was unanswerable; it was true. And it was natural that Filomena should think more of her uncle than of Richard, whom she had never seen.

She thought of saying, "I am sorry I could not pay you," but it seemed to her that it would be an insult. Filomena might be mercenary, she had admitted as much in that revealing sentence about a reward, but Don Luigi was not.

She said, "Look. You can have this ring. I am afraid it isn't worth very much, but it might fetch a few lire. It is mine. I can part with it. It belonged to my mother—"

Filomena took it grudgingly, without a word of thanks, and her voice was no less hostile when she said, "You shouldn't have come here. People will talk and wonder. A young lady like you shouldn't be wandering about the town alone. I don't know what Donna Amalia can be thinking of to allow it—unless she wants you to get into trouble. That may be it. My uncle let himself be involved. He's too kindhearted. But that's finished. Sorry. You're only sorry because you can't make use of him any more."

"That isn't true," cried Alda—and yet there was some truth in it. She had come meaning to ask Filomena if she could take food up to Richard in his hiding-place, or if she knew anyone who could be trusted to take her uncle's place.

"I will try to make other arrangements," she said with a little air of dignity that made Filomena look at her with surprise, for she had expected an emotional storm. "He—he has been five days, I suppose, without provisions?"

Filomena answered glumly, "Since last Saturday."

"I will find someone, or go there myself. Will you tell me how to find the place?"

"I don't know. I have never been there."

"But you must have some idea. Didn't Don Luigi ever talk about it? He was so proud of his discovery. I know he kept it a secret, but you, living with him—"

"He never told me. I should not have been interested. I do not like the woods. I am afraid of snakes. You must go as you please, signorina, but I advise you for your own sake to do nothing more in this affair. It is dangerous."

"I cannot leave a fellow creature to die of starvation."

"He won't die. He'll fend for himself one way or another. Why should you feel yourself responsible?"

"I can't leave him," said Alda steadily.

Filomena shrugged her shoulders and said, in her flat little voice, "Of course. All that scribbling. You fancy yourself in love. I have warned you. I cannot do more. Only one thing. Whatever happens you won't bring my name or my uncle's into the affair."

"I can promise you that."

"Then you will go now. And please do not come again."

Alda looked at her wonderingly. So this was what Filomena was like when her uncle's influence was removed. No rock to lean on here, only crumbling clay.

"Don't be afraid," she said. "I won't. *Addio*, Filomena."

It was hot on the road-going back to the villa. All this had taken time, and she would be very late for the midday meal.

Old Pietro was coming out of the dining-room as she crossed the hall.

"I was clearing away, and just going to bring the coffee. Where have you been, signorina? Donna Amalia is angry—"

Alda felt she could not face a scolding from la Marucci. It was not only that she was tired, her throat ached with unshed tears, she felt confused and frightened. "Tell her I have a headache and have gone to my room to lie down."

"*Bene.* I will bring you a cup of black coffee." He shuffled away with his laden tray and she went on up the stairs, wearily, with dragging feet.

Presently, when she had changed her frock and rested, she would go up the hill to the podere. She had not seen the baby for two days and she wanted to talk to Marietta. There was something solid and comfortable about Marietta. She might be ignorant, but she had a fund of natural wisdom and kindliness. She might not be able to help, but she would not turn on a friend.

Chiara brought up the coffee and sat on the foot of the bed while Alda drank it.

"You need not tell me you've been all this time confessing. Really, Alda, you go too far. You are giving that woman some reason to complain of your conduct to the marchese. Don't you know she's dying to do just that and persuade him to send you away as not fit company for me?"

"I thought you were going to get rid of her first."

But the malicious joy Chiara had felt when she first read her letter from Venice had had time to evaporate. She was fundamentally too lazy and too timid to face any unpleasantness that could be avoided. "As to that I may not do anything. She's not so bad really. She's been quite pleasant to me lately. You heard what she said the other day about having the baby weaned as soon as possible. After all. I'm only nineteen. The marchese would have to put some older person in charge here. He might find someone who insisted on sitting with us and reading aloud from dull devotional works. At least we are spared that."

Alda laughed a little. It was so like Chiara to start some-thing and then lose interest. Alda smiled at her with indulgent amusement. No one could be too critical of Chiara's whims and fancies. She was so lovely to look at. No wonder poor Amedeo had worshipped her as he did.

"About this morning," she said. "I had to make my confes-sion to a stranger. He told me Don Luigi had had a stroke. I went to the hospital to see him. He's very ill, paralysed and practically speechless. Then I went on to visit Filom-ena, to ask if there was anything we could do, but she said not. That is why I was late. You might tell Donna Amalia if she speaks of it again to you, Chiara."

"I will. And I'm so sorry about poor old Don Luigi. But how enterprising of you to go to the hospital all by yourself. I should never have dared."

Alda sat up. She had accounted satisfactorily for her time, and she did not want to have to answer further ques-tions. "If I am going up to the podere this afternoon I must get ready."

She went over to the washstand to bathe her face, and ran a comb through her curls.

Chiara watched her stepping into a little sleeveless frock of amber-coloured silk which had been hers until she got tired of it. "I wish I was well enough to climb the hill," she said wistfully, "it's silly to be so short of breath."

"You'll be stronger in a year or two, *cara*. The doctor said so."

"I'll go with you as far as the vineyard," said Chiara. Alda would rather have gone alone. Chiara walked so slowly and could not be hurried. But she would not dissuade, her, and presently they were walking along the path by the ilex hedge, and Chiara, laughing gaily, was mimicking the croaking of frogs in the lily pool. She leaned rather heavily, though, on her cousin's arm, and Alda thought she looked pale.

"You have come far enough." She turned impulsively to the elder girl and kissed her with unusual warmth. Later she was to remember that moment and be glad of it, even though it wrung her heart. "Go back to the house now and rest."

Chiara smiled at her. "Very well, Granny. What should I do without you? If I do have another baby and it is a girl, I shall call her Alda. Kiss my little Giovannino for me." When Alda was alone there was no need to pretend to be cheerful, and she could concentrate her mind on her worries. As she hurried along the dusty track between the vines laden with their bunches of unripe grapes she was thinking of Richard Drew lying in his unknown and inaccessible hiding-place and slowly starving to death. It was a horrible picture, but she could not put it from her. Such things had happened. Stories came back to her that she had read and forgotten, stories of fugitives shut up in secret rooms and forgotten until their bones were found years later, of nuns walled up alive, of Ugolino and his sons in the Tower of Famine.

It was very hot, but she was hardly aware of it, though sweat was trickling down her face and between her shoulder blades, under the thin silk. "I must do something," she thought, "what can I do?"

CHAPTER VII

DEATH AT THE VILLA

MARIETTA was sitting on the steps of the podere, knitting stockings of coarse unbleached wool, and leaning forward occasionally to rock the wooden cradle in which her foster child lay asleep. The old charcoal burner and his wife were away in the woods gathering fuel.

Alda sat down by her, panting, and fanning herself with her hat.

"You should not have climbed the hill so fast in the heat of the day, signorina."

"I know. But I wanted to talk to you—" she told Marietta about Don Luigi's stroke and Filomena's change of front and her anxiety about their protégé.

"What shall we do, Mari?"

The peasant girl shook her sleek black head. "Nothing, signorina. There is nothing we can do."

"Your father knows these woods. Couldn't he find the hiding-place?"

"He only knows the woods that belong to the marchese. But do not be too unhappy, *signorina mia*," she added quickly. "He was ill when we found him, but you say he has recovered. He is not a child, or helpless. He will fend for himself. *Fara da se.*"

"I hope you are right," sighed Alda.

"If he is good the saints will look after him," said Marietta.

Alda did not feel so sure of that, but did not care to argue the point. She bent forward to brush a fly off the sleeping child's cheek. "He is quite well?"

"The signorina can see for herself," said Marietta proudly. "He is growing fat and strong as a little lion. Shall I bring him down to the Villa one day so that the marchesina can see him?"

She looked disappointed when Alda said that Donna Amalia thought it inadvisable. It might have an unsettling effect on Chiara, who would not like parting from him. The child was to be weaned in the autumn, and she could have him then for good.

"I shall miss him," said Marietta sadly, "but the signori know best."

"Your husband will be coming home, and you will have another baby of your own."

"I hope so," she said simply, "but it is a long time since we heard from Domenico. Sometimes I am afraid. He did not want to fight. He wanted to work as he had always done in the fields, and help my father, and stay with me."

It was time to go back to the Villa.

Alda had been vaguely comforted by Marietta's child-like faith, but she could not really resign herself to doing nothing. If she prayed hard enough, and to the right saints, perhaps she would be shown a way. The question of to whom she was to address her petitions occupied her mind as she went down the hill again by the winding dusty path between the vines. Saint Richard perhaps, after whom he was named, and Saint George, the patron of England. "But I don't know anything about them," she thought, "and they won't know me. It will be safer to ask the Madonna. She is always kind. She will understand—"

The walls of the Villa were honey-coloured in the warm light of the setting sun, and some of the windows, where the shutters had been thrown back, gleamed like jewels. The house, like the gardens, had been neglected for many years. There had been no money since the end of the eighteenth century, either for carpenters to make repairs or for numerous servants, indoors or out. Stucco and paint were peeling, the stone of the balustrades was crumbling. In two thirds of the rooms spiders spun their webs and birds built their nests in the chimneys. But the Villa remained impressive, with the indestructible beauty of perfect proportions, still able, in its decline, to touch the hearts of those who care for such things. Even Alda, who had never been happy under that roof, found herself admiring the place at certain moments and feeling proud that Chiara's baby would inherit its faded glories.

The southern twilight is very short. The sunset gold had faded to green and grey and the fireflies were already sparkling among the rose bushes when she entered the house. There was no one on the terrace, but there was a light in the *salotto*. Alda looked in on her way upstairs, expecting to find Chiara, but Donna Amalia was there alone. She was writing a letter, but looked up as the door opened.

"Ah, it's you, Alda. The baby is well? It is really very good of you to trudge up that hill three times a week as you do," she said with unexpected amiability. "If you were the child's aunt instead of only a second cousin you could not be more devoted. Come in, *cara*, and shut the door after you. There is a draught."

"I ought to go up now to change before supper—"

"Ah, supper. I am afraid—the fact is we've had some trouble while you have been out. An accident—"

Alda's heart seemed to miss a beat and then to make up for it by thudding against her ribs. "Chiara—" she began.

"No. No." Donna Amalia laid down her pen and lit a cigarette. She always smoked her cigarettes in a long red holder. "It was Caterina. She was taking clean towels out of the linen chest upstairs. There was a scorpion and the creature stung her. The doctor has been and gone again. I sent Pietro to fetch him. Her arm is black and swollen up to the shoulder. She is to remain in bed until the inflammation has abated. Pietro is sitting with her. He is a most devoted husband. Meanwhile, we shall have to depend for service on the girl Romilda. She is a fool, but I suppose she will be able to make coffee, and, for the rest, we must live on bread and cheese and salads and fruit. And you can make yourself useful perhaps."

"I will do what I can," said Alda. "Where is Chiara?"

"She was upset by the fuss and excitement, hearing Caterina screaming. She has gone to bed. You can take her up some supper on a tray. Find out what she fancies." She picked up her pen to indicate that the audience was over.

A quarter of an hour later, Alda knocked gently at her cousin's door. A bath and a change of clothing had refreshed her, and she felt more or less able to cope with her new duties. She was sorry for Caterina, but the emergency took her mind off her own private troubles. She found that Chiara had undressed and got into bed, but she was not asleep, and she looked rather flushed and feverish.

"You have heard what happened," she said excitedly, "a scorpion. I've always been terrified of them. I made Romilda strip this bed and look in all the corners and poke a broom under the chest of drawers and the wardrobe—"

"They don't often come indoors," said Alda. "I expect the towels were laid out on the grass to bleach, and the creature got entangled in the crochet edging of one of them and was brought in when they were folded. Caterina's eyesight isn't very good. Don't worry, *cara*. It isn't likely to happen again."

"She won't die, will she?"

"Of course not. She'll be back in the kitchen in a few days."

"You're such a comfort," sighed Chiara, settling down among her pillows. "How is the child?"

"Very well. Donna Amalia has asked me to look after you, so tell me what you want for supper and I'll see what can be done about it."

Chiara reflected. "It's so hot. I'm not hungry. A small piece of bread. Crusty. You know I love crusts. A slice of ricotta and a few radishes, and a glass of wine."

Alda looked doubtful. "Radishes are indigestible."

"*Macche!* They never hurt me."

"Very well."

Romilda was in the kitchen doing some ironing. She was a thick set and rather vacant-looking young woman, who was a willing worker but had to be told what to do. Alda sent her into the vegetable garden to pull lettuces and radishes for a salad while she prepared two trays, one for Chiara and the other for the dining-room. When, presently, she and Donna Amalia sat down to their supper it was not much past the usual hour.

Donna Amalia, who was still in a surprisingly good humour, congratulated her. "Cold sausage, ricotta, salted anchovies, an excellent salad. You have done very well. To-morrow you must try your hand at an omelette. If Caterina does not recover we might ask the marchese to keep you on as cook," she said, with her cold little laugh. It was one of those double edged remarks she was apt to make which might or might not be meant to be offensive.

Alda managed to smile. "Wait until you've eaten the omelette. I'll clear away and help Romilda wash up, and then, if there isn't anything else you want done, I'll go to bed. I'm rather tired."

Donna Amalia was lighting a cigarette. "I should," she said when she had blown out the match. "You have had a busy day. I shall sit on the terrace for a while. Pietro will lock up as usual at eleven. Don't forget Chiara's lemonade. She always drinks some when she wakes up in the night."

Alda had forgotten, and she was glad to be reminded. "How does Caterina make it? Do you know?"

Donna Amalia was just going out by the french window, a slight elegant figure in the black satin frock that had come from one of the best dress shops in Rome and was cut after a Paris model. Her high-heeled slippers of crimson brocade matched her cigarette-holder, her lips and nails. Lately she had been dressing very carefully every evening as if she expected visitors. She glanced back over her shoulder. "The usual way, I suppose," she said curtly, "one lemon, a spoonful of honey, hot water."

There was no sign of Romilda in the kitchen, and the back door was ajar. Alda guessed that the girl had taken the opportunity to slip out to meet her *fidanzato* who was the under-gardener at the Villa. She made the lemonade and took it up to Chiara's room.

Chiara was asleep, and she was careful not to disturb her, setting the glass down on the bedside table and creeping out again.

She had been on her feet during the greater part of the day, and she had been under a continuous emotional strain, and she was mentally and physically exhausted. She stepped out of her clothes, leaving them lying on the floor in defiance of all the rules of the convent, and almost fell into bed, and she was sleeping almost before her head touched the pillow.

She woke with a start some hours later with confused recollections of a dream. It had something to do with Donna Amalia's new dress. It suited her, she looked ten years younger in it, but it was hardly the sort of creation that would be chosen by a widowed gentlewoman occupying a responsible position in a nobleman's household. It was such a dress as she might have worn in her role of hostess in the private gambling hell in the Canale San Gregorio. It had been imprudent to buy it, and still more imprudent to wear it at the Villa. Her only excuse was that after more than three years of playing an irksome part she was sick to death of dowdy respectability. In any case there had only been Alda, that convent bred little ninny, to see her.

But Alda had instincts that made up for her lack of worldly experience; she often knew without being able to say how she knew. There had been something unpleasant, something frightening in her dream, a signal set at Danger, red as la Marucci's high-heeled slippers. Red as—

She had been awakened, though she had not realised it, by a sound in the next room. Now she heard it again. A moaning whimpering sound of an animal in pain. She jumped out of bed, switched on her light and reached for her bedroom slippers. The corridor was in darkness. She felt for the handle of Chiara's door, turned it and went in. Chiara was sitting huddled up on the side of her bed. Her bedside lamp was alight. There was vomit on the floor and on the disordered bedclothes and the sheets and her blue silk pyjamas were stained with blood. She looked up at Alda as she came in. Her eyes were red rimmed and dilated with terror.

"Alda—I feel awful. Help me. Do something—"

She began to retch. Alda held her until the paroxysm abated and she relaxed and lay back exhausted in the younger girl's arms.

"Listen, *amore*," Alda tried to keep her voice steady. "I must leave you just for a minute. I must get Donna Amalia. Pietro will fetch the doctor. He will give you something. Oh, my sweet, don't be frightened. You'll be better soon—"

Chiara made no reply. Her eyes were closed. Alda lowered her gently on to the pillows and hurried out of the room. As she ran down the long corridor to Donna Amalia's room at the far end her thoughts were in a turmoil. Was it a miscarriage? Or those radishes? Donna Amalia would know what to do. Clean sheets. Hot water. Pietro to be roused and sent into the town for the doctor. They were not on the telephone. The marchese disliked modern inventions though Alda remembered Amedeo laughing and saying that his father had one in his flat in Rome. No car, not even a bicycle. Perhaps, she thought, she should go instead of Pietro, he was old and slow, and she could run part of the way.

She knocked on Donna Amalia's door. A voice said sharply, "What is it?"

"It is me, Alda. Chiara has been sick. She is ill, very ill—"

"Wait a minute. I'll come."

Donna Amalia did not keep her waiting long though she had put on a dressing-gown and tied a silk scarf over her head. She asked a few matter-of-fact questions as they went along the corridor together. Alda offered to go for the doctor instead of Pietro.

"Certainly not. Go and wake him up now. Tell him to hurry. Wake Romilda too. Tell her to light the fire in the kitchen and put on kettles. Be quick. Then come back to me. I shall probably need your help."

Pietro fortunately had not gone to bed or taken off his clothes. He was dozing in a chair by his wife's bedside, and within a few minutes of being roused he was on his way. Caterina, who had been given a sedative, was not disturbed. Romilda, a heavy sleeper, was aroused at last and went stumbling down from her garret, her dress unbuttoned and her coarse black hair hanging about her face, to light the fire.

Alda hurried back to Chiara's room. She was dreading what she might find there, but Chiara was lying quietly in the bed. Donna Amalia said there had been another crisis, but it had passed.

"She rests in between, but each time she is weaker. I don't understand it. I have bathed her face and hands. Put the soiled linen out in the passage and bring clean sheets. We must try to make her more comfortable." Donna Amalia was calm and efficient. "I'm used to illness," she said. "I nursed the marchesa through her last illness. One must have order."

She looked shrewdly at Alda who had sat down rather suddenly. "You feel faint? I am not surprised. It is the shock. I will give you a dose of sal volatile. You will lie down on your bed for ten minutes. Then you may come back. You are no use to me as you are."

"You'll call me if—"

"I will."

Alda drank the milky fluid Donna Amalia had poured into a glass, walked rather uncertainly into her room and lay down on her bed.

Chapter VIII
THE CRIME AND THE MOTIVE

Don Gaetano Gualtieri, marchese di Mont Alvino, was a man of distinguished appearance. His tall, lean, rather rigid figure, his long, narrow face with the melancholy dark eyes and the little pointed beard, black streaked with silver, bore a strong resemblance to the portrait of an ancestor painted by El Greco that hung in the library at the Villa, a room that was never used in his absence. He sat there now at the head of the table on which his meals were sometimes served when he chose to eat alone. His lawyer, Taddeo Bianchi, who had accompanied him from Rome, sat on his right hand, and Donna Amalia on his left. Facing them were Doctor Sartini, and two Government officials, the prefetto and his secretary.

The doctor was a youngish man, sallow faced, with bags under his eyes, and a weak mouth not hidden by a small, waxed moustache.

"I am sorry," he said, "but there is no doubt about it. I got here soon after three o'clock, and she was sinking then. I did everything possible. It may be some consolation to you to know that the end was quite peaceful."

"But she had suffered before," said the marchese harshly.

"She suffered. Yes."

"She called for help?"

"It seems so. Her cousin, Signorina Alda Olivieri, who occupied the adjoining room, heard her and went to her. She then fetched Donna Amalia, who sent a servant to fetch me. Donna Amalia, if she will allow me to say so, was admirable in this emergency, a most capable and devoted nurse—"

The marchese looked at her with the shadow of a smile. "I know. During my late wife's illness she was an angel of compassion." From him the phrase did not sound too high flown. The prefetto and his secretary looked impressed. Signor Bianchi stroked his chin. "After a while, I understand, Alda Olivieri complained of being tired and sleepy. Donna Amalia was, I think, a little surprised that she should be thinking of herself at such a moment but she sent her to her room to lie down and, strange as it may seem, she was so little affected by what she had seen and heard that she went to sleep and slept for the remainder of the night. I can bear witness to that for it was I who woke her."

They all looked at the secretary who was making notes. The prefetto cleared his throat. "When were your suspicions first aroused?"

"Almost immediately. I had thought of a duodenal ulcer, but Donna Amalia told me the marchesina had an excellent digestion, and I had never treated her for any trouble of that sort. She was delicate. She was anaemic and her heart was not strong, but otherwise there was nothing wrong. Alda Olivieri told me this morning that her cousin believed herself to be *incinta*, but that was a mistake. She was not. Perhaps she herself was doubtful for she seems to have said nothing about it to Donna Amalia. To resume—while I was still trying to save her I had no time, naturally, for speculation, but when—when it was over—I acknowledged some very unpleasant doubts. I asked for jars and collected specimens of the vomit and the blood—forgive me, Donna Amalia, this is very painful—" She had covered her face with her hands. She murmured, "No. Don't mind me. Go on—"

"I enquired as to what she had eaten and drunk not long before the attack. I had been called in yesterday afternoon to attend the cook who had been stung by a scorpion and I knew that meals must have been disorganised. Donna Amalia told me that the marchesina had gone to bed early and her supper had been taken up to her on a tray. The supper was prepared and served by Alda Olivieri. The marchesina always had a glass of lemonade on the table by her bed at night and she usually drank some if not all of it. On this occasion the lemonade was prepared by Olivieri. No one saw her do it as the servant girl Romilda admits that she had gone down to the end of the avenue to meet her *fidanzato* and was away from the house for about an hour. The glass was still standing on the night table. There was about a spoonful of liquid at the bottom of the glass. I noticed some sediment. I took away the glass and the other specimens and with the assistance of a colleague at the hospital I made some preliminary tests. A further analysis will be made but the reactions left no doubt in our minds. Your daughter-in-law, signor marchese, died of arsenical poisoning."

"I can't believe it," said Donna Amalia huskily, "it is too terrible."

"'There is the question of motive," said the lawyer, speaking for the first time. "I always understood that the marchesina was greatly attached to her cousin, who had been brought up with her and that it was at her express wish that she was living here."

The marchese answered. "That is so. My son was much away and Chiara needed her cousin's company. Amedeo liked her, I believe. I am seldom here. Since the death of my wife and of my son I find it too full of memories. Donna Amalia will be able to tell you whether the two girls were on good terms."

They all looked at her as she seemed to hesitate. "They always used to be. Until quite recently. But I have noticed a change in Alda. She was restless. She went to market sometimes in the morning with the cook. That seemed harmless, but she did not always come back with her. I blame myself now for not being more strict, but—I was responsible for Chiara's well-being, but not or not directly, for that of her cousin. Only a few days ago I overheard Chiara say something to her—I forget the exact words but the suggestion was that Alda was doing something of which Chiara did not approve. Yesterday Alda went ostensibly to confession, but she was out the whole morning and she did not appear at lunch. Chiara was worried, I could see, and she went up to her cousin's room to speak to her. I don't know what passed between them but I heard raised voices as if they were quarrelling. If they were, they made it up for when Alda went up to the podere later to see the baby, Chiara walked a little way with her. I saw them from my window. Chiara was so sweet-tempered that she could never be angry long."

"All this is rather vague, Donna Amalia," said the lawyer. "Have you any theory? I mean—what do you suppose they were quarrelling about?"

"I believe that Alda has been carrying on a clandestine love affair, and that Chiara may have threatened to tell me if it went any further. But that is not to say I believe Alda would—no, that is incredible."

The marchese's face was like granite. He looked across the table at the prefetto. "What action have you taken?" The prefetto had been listening attentively as a producer might to a run through of a play. "She has been kept in her room all day while I questioned the servants. You have heard the evidence summarised. It seemed to me sufficient, but naturally there must be further enquiries. I had her removed half an hour before you arrived. She will be kept apart from the other prisoners and well looked after. After all, as Donna Amalia says, we must not jump to conclusions."

"Donna Amalia's kind heart does her credit," said the marchese, "but I cannot regard a poisoner as an object for compassion."

Looking at him they all realised his suppressed fury. The old lawyer, who knew him best, ventured to lay a hand on his arm. "It is not yet proved."

The marchese ignored him. "What does she say?"

The prefetto answered. "The doctor and Donna Amalia were with her when I arrived soon after eight o'clock. I was accompanied by Major Ansaldo, of the Carabinieri, and several subordinates. The doctor joined us and informed us of what had taken place and of his suspicions. He had the specimens and the glass that had held the lemonade ready for removal. After we had viewed the room and taken some photographs the body was taken away for the post mortem examination which took place later. As the signor marchese knows according to our law the funeral must take place within twenty-four hours of death taking place, but a few hours grace are allowed for convenience. The interment will be to-morrow morning at seven in the Gualtieri chapel at the Duomo. The vault is being opened and all arrangements made for the ceremony. Carriages will call at the Villa for the family and other mourners at half-past six. May I take this opportunity to offer the signor marchese the sincere condolences of his tenants and his fellow citizens of Mont Alvino in this, his second bereavement within a few months."

The marchese thanked him with a stiff bow. The prefetto, who had delivered his little speech in a hesitating and deferential manner, sat back and mopped his hot face before he resumed.

"At the doctor's request Donna Amalia had remained with the suspect while she was dressing and while the police routine was being carried out. I then saw her and put some questions to her, Donna Amalia, the doctor, and my secretary being present. She was not crying but she was pale and appeared to be dazed, though she answered my questions clearly and without hesitation.

"Briefly, she said that she had heard her cousin crying out and had gone to her. Seeing that she was very ill she had gone at once to fetch Donna Amalia. She had imagined that some radishes the marchesina ate for supper might have disagreed with her. She admitted that she had prepared the supper and had made the lemonade, and that she was alone in the kitchen at the time. She denied having put any sort of powder in the food or the drink. The lemonade was sweetened with honey. She denied having quarrelled with her cousin. There had been no dispute or ill feeling. She had no secret and nothing to hide. She could not tell me the name of her lover. She had no lover. I asked Donna Amalia to be good enough to go down to the dining-room with the suspect and remain with her while she had some breakfast. We then carried out a thorough search of her room. A paper packet, opened, and containing a little white powder, was found under the handkerchiefs in a silk sachet at the back of the drawer in which she kept her gloves and scarves. It was tied up and sealed with my seal before being taken away for analysis. The doctor thought it was arsenic, and he was right. That is our case so far. I think you will agree that it justified me in making an arrest."

"It is terrible," murmured Donna Amalia, "how could she!"

"Love," said the prefetto didactically, "has a devastating effect on some young people. I can remember many cases in the criminal records of young men and young women who murdered relatives who obstructed the course of a love affair. There was a famous trial in Rome, in 1903, I think, of a youth who killed his mother and got rid of the body by degrees because she would not give her consent to his marriage with some girl. I have forgotten the details, but there were some charred bones—"

Signor Bianchi coughed. "*Scusi*. This is hardly the moment. You will distress the signora—"

Donna Amalia had shown no signs of distress, but she took the hint and shuddered.

Silvio Manicci was lounging in a wicker chair on the terrace, waiting for his mother to join him. He had not seen her alone since his arrival. He had brought the marchese and his lawyer from Rome in his car, the car for which he was still able to get petrol, thanks to his connections with the Fascist Party, and he would be driving them back after the funeral.

The marchese had told Donna Amalia that her son had been invaluable, tactful, sympathetic, self-effacing. Silvio had overheard and been satisfied. He had been quick to see that it would be useless to try and make a good impression on the old gentleman in his son's life time. Amedeo had never liked him and would soon have put a stop to any attempts he might have made to ingratiate himself. But now the field was open. He would have to be careful though. The marchese's attitude to the Government was correct, but chilly. He professed no interest in politics and really knew little about them or he could hardly have failed to learn that Silvio was a pet of some of the Party bosses.

Silvio lit another cigarette and turned his head to watch his mother come out of the library and move towards him. She walked well, he thought, she held herself well. *Diamine!* what a woman!

He rose with his usual languid grace and set a chair for her next to his own. She took a cigarette from his proffered case.

They smoked in silence for a minute. Then he said, "Quite a clearance of the board. Pim. Pam. They are swept off left and right. But what will you do, *mamma mia*, you, the model duenna? Whose virtue is there to safeguard now?"

"The marchese is very kind. He has asked me to make the Villa my home for the present."

"What happened exactly?"

"The police theory is that Chiara discovered that her cousin was involved with some man, that she threatened to tell me about it, and that Alda poisoned her to prevent the affair from coming to light."

Silvio took his cigarette from his mouth and examined the lighted end with great apparent interest. "I said—what happened exactly?"

"How should I know? But she is in love, Silvio. There's no doubt about that. One can always tell."

"Who is the man?"

"I have no idea. It must be someone she picked up in the town. I have not been able to find out. The servants may know, but it's no use asking them. They don't like me. It hardly matters. The police will look for him, I suppose, but if he's not a fool he will make himself scarce. It may be a compliment to have your mistress committing murders on your account, but it can be inconvenient. The point is that it gives her a motive."

"Adequate—you think?"

Donna Amalia smiled. "The prefetto thinks so. He was quite amusing on the subject."

"So—there's nothing to worry about?"

She hesitated. "I wouldn't say that. There was a letter. I overheard—Chiara had a letter from Venice—a few days ago—"

Silvio whistled. "Full of news?"

"Yes. And I haven't been able to find it—yet. I shall eventually. The marchese has asked me to go over her things. The little cat had claws."

"I see. And have the police any theory about how Alda came by the poison? What was it?"

"The doctor says arsenic." She looked at Silvio. "You think that is important?"

"It might be. They are bound to wonder about it sooner or later. Many things can be bought if you have money and know where to go, but Alda had none. Of course, there is almost certain to be a crooked chemist or herbalist in Mont Alvino, one of those kind-hearted fellows who help women out of their troubles—"

Donna Amalia slightly shook her head. "They use an arsenical compound to spray the vines in the spring for the phylloxera. We all saw it being done. There might be some left in a tin in one of the outbuildings. She passes it every time she goes up to the podere."

"Has that been brought to their notice?"

"Not yet."

"Give them a little time. It might be better if they found it for themselves."

"If I do make the suggestion," said Donna Amalia, "it will be with the utmost reluctance. They know that, in spite of everything, I cannot bring myself to believe in her guilt."

Glancing at him she saw that he was shaking with suppressed laughter.

She said sharply, "Be careful. Here he is. And he's not blind. We must not underestimate him—"

The marchese had come out of the library, but he did not join them. He crossed the terrace and went down the steps. They watched him going up the long pleached walk by the ilex hedge.

"Where is he going?"

"Up to the podere probably to see his grandson."

"To be sure," said Silvio sleepily, "the grandson. What devotion after a long and tiring day. I am to drive him and Bianchi in to Mont Alvino to dine at the Hotel Leon Bianco this evening. It was his idea, to save you trouble as the cook is ill. They will sleep at the Villa. You will be able to provide rolls and coffee in the morning?"

"Of course." She added unexpectedly, "I shall be glad when it is over. I do not like funerals. What's that?"

His chair grated on the pavement as he turned to look. He had been startled by her expression as she leaned forward to stare at something behind him.

"Nothing. They often sat there by the lily pool about this hour of the day. For a moment I almost thought—it was an illusion, an effect of light—"

"You are over-tired," he said coolly, "that is all."

CHAPTER IX
RICHARD MEETS A FRIEND

THE sun had not risen to disperse the morning mists, but the housewives of Mont Alvino liked to do their shopping

early. Old Pellico's nephew had taken down the shutters
and was sprinkling the narrow pavement outside the shop
with a watering-can, whistling as he worked and occasionally glancing up, with a grin, at his cousin Tonietta, whose
tousled black head was visible at an upper window. One of
his feet was wrapped up in dingy bandages and he leaned
on a crutch. Later in the day when there were more people
about he would have to remain in the dark and stuffy back
room, but for the present he was safe enough. He set down
the empty can, helped himself to a handful of cherries from
a basket behind the shop counter and sat down on the doorstep to eat them.

A shabby and dishevelled figure came uncertainly round
the corner and edged its way along, pausing rather frequently
to lean against the house walls. Drunk as a lord, thought
young Pellico. Drunk at five o'clock in the morning. His
eyes narrowed and grew wary as the man came nearer. He
wore the blue linen trousers and coarse homespun shirt of
a farm labourer and his head was bare. Pellico stared hard
at that tangled mop of thick fair hair. He spat out the last
of the cherry stones, reached for his crutch and stood up.

"Drew—"

The haggard bearded face was turned blindly towards
him, the sunken blue eyes unfocused. He seized the man's
arm and was horrified to feel nothing but skin and bone.

"It's all right," he said urgently, "don't be afraid, mate.
Come in here—"

Tonietta came running down the stairs. "Who is it, Aristide?"

"A friend. Help me get him into the back room. That's
better. Look, Toni, he's not drunk. There's no smell of liquor.

He's been sleeping rough by the look of things, and with nothing to eat. Is there any milk?"

"Not a drop."

"Wine then, and a slice of bread. Stir your stumps, Fatty."

Tonietta, not in the least hurt by this ungallant reference to her generous curves, stood by, with her hands on her hips, staring with mingled curiosity and compassion while Aristide very gently and carefully fed his patient, whom he had laid on his own bed, with bits of bread soaked in wine.

"That's enough for the present, buddy. You've got to go slow, see. A bit of shut eye and then we'll talk—"

He stood for a moment watching, and then, beckoning to his cousin to follow, tip-toed out of the room.

His uncle, a little wizened man with the wrinkled brown face of a monkey, was waiting for them in the shop.

Customers would be arriving before long and all three watched the shop door anxiously as they talked in whispers.

"Who is it, Aristide?"

"One of the crew of the plane. I made sure they were all killed. Maybe he baled out in time. He must have done, for the plane crashed, and I saw the glow in the sky. He must have been hiding in the woods. God knows how he kept himself alive for over three weeks. Lucky for him he came down this street just when I was about."

His uncle grunted. "That remains to be seen. You have your papers, and you are one of us. Even if they searched the house and found you here your story might hold together. But to hide an English airman means a firing party, or so they say."

"Don't worry," said his nephew cheerfully. "It will only be for a few days. My ankle is healing nicely, and he only needs feeding up. A few bowls of your good chestnut soup,

Toni—look out, here's someone to buy an ounce of the sheep's milk cheese—"

He slipped into the back room leaving Toni and her father to mind the shop.

When Richard woke a few hours later he was fully conscious, though still very weak and feeling the pangs of hunger. He was lying on a frowsy camp bed in an untidy kitchen. A plump young woman with a mass of dishevelled black hair was sitting by the stove shelling broad beans into a pan. She grinned at him good-naturedly when he caught her eye. A young man dressed like himself in blue linen trousers and a shirt open at the throat, was sitting by his bedside. He, too, smiled expansively as Richard looked at him.

"Look who's here," he said.

Richard drew a long breath. "Pellico. I've been wondering. What happened? I haven't heard—"

He stopped, for Pellico's expressive face had conveyed a warning.

"Okay," he said. "It doesn't matter while you talk English. She doesn't understand. I haven't been able to get round to doing the job yet, see. I've got the doings safely hidden. The trouble is I damaged my ankle. Not a chance of getting away to the coast hopping on one foot with a crutch. I might have risked that, though I'm no blooming hero, but I got to get to the place first, see, and as things are I can't hire no taxi, nor get pushed in a bath-chair or a pram. Well, how are you feeling now, mate? Cor, you could have knocked me down with a feather when you come staggering down the street this morning. What about the others?"

"I was the only one who got clear. Fire broke out at once. I can't remember much about it. I must have been stunned, I suppose. I started walking. I walked for hours, and then I must have crawled for a bit. Some people from a farm found me. They dug a hole and buried my uniform—my flying kit—"

Toni had left her beans to stir some thick brown stew in a pot on the stove. She poured some into a basin.

"Not so much talk," she commanded. "Here, you—what is his name, Aristide?"

"You can call him Ricardo."

Richard enjoyed the stew though he felt it might be better not to enquire too closely into its components.

He knew that he had been incredibly lucky in finding another haven. He had left his hiding place in the woods v after five days without food because he had realised that if he waited any longer he would almost certainly die there. As it was, he had only just managed to struggle down the hill side. Once on the road the going had been easier, and again he had been lucky for the town gate had just been opened to admit the first market cart and he had passed in unnoticed while the *dogana* officials were busy. But he had formed no plan. Sooner or later, he supposed, he would be arrested. What would happen after that he did not know, nor did he much care, but he hoped they would give him something to eat.

The kitchen behind Pellico's shop was hot and airless. The only window opened on a blank wall. Fleas hopped about on the brick floor, and any food left on the table was instantly covered with flies. But after the deathly silence and solitude of the Etruscan tomb it seemed cheerful and home-like. He was impressed by the easy going good nature of the old man and his daughter and by their apparent indifference to danger. He saw little of them for they both had to be in the shop serving customers, but he had Aristide for company, and Aristide had a great fund of conversation.

Aristide's father had been one of three brothers. The eldest had carried on the family business in Mont Alvino, the second had gone to America, and the youngest had found his way to London, where, after working for some years as a waiter, he had married the daughter of his employer and helped him run a little Italian restaurant in Soho. Aristide was born there, the eldest of seven children.

"Three brothers and three sisters, Pia, Carmela, and Aurelia. I wish you could have seen them, pal. They were good lookers. Easy on the eye. I was in the Air Force, see. In Blackpool at the time, taking a course. No Isle of Man stuff for us. Il Babbo had been naturalised. And we all loved England and had no use for the black shirt crowd, though we had to be careful, see, because some of our neighbours thought different."

Aristide looked like an Italian, but his voice when he talked English was the voice of London, of the London that goes to the pictures and acquires the vocabulary of the celluloid gangster.

"In Blackpool, see, that time Soho Square copped it. You remember. Where our place was—just a heap of rubble. The house where I was born and—and everybody in it."

"Tough," murmured Richard.

Aristide was silent for a while. Then he said, "Maybe if I get through the war I'll team up with uncle and Toni here, or get them over to England. Toni—you couldn't call her svelte, but she's comfortable."

"They don't know what you are here for?"

"No." He was sitting on the floor massaging his ankle. "I'll be fit for action by the end of the week," he said. "The line is a mile or more out of the town, but you can hear the trains when the wind's the right way. I've noticed the troop trains seem to pass in the early morning. If we could blow one up with the bridge, eh?" He licked his lips. "Perhaps after that I'd stop dreaming. It's always the same dream. A mountain of broken bricks and charred beams and just one hand sticking out. Carmela's little brown hand with a ring on it she got out of a cracker that last Christmas. Carmela. She was always laughing. The jolliest kid you ever saw. She was my best pal. I'd like to get ten Jerries, a hundred Jerries, for each finger on that hand," he said savagely.

"Maybe you will." Richard tried to think of something consoling to say. "The world's in a bloody mess, and it will take years to clear up the pieces. Life isn't going to be easy even after the war. Your little sister may be happier where she is. Happy and safe."

That evening old Pellico went to play bowls with his friends on a dusty patch of ground under some plane trees just outside the nearest town gate. When he came home he brought news.

The shop was closed, and Tonietta was sitting with the two young men in the kitchen looking on while Aristide taught the Englishman the national game of Morra.

"Look. I throw my hand out so. With three fingers up. I have to guess how many fingers you will put up at the same time, and you too. We both call the result before we are quite sure. *Cinque! Sei!* Ah, here is *lo zio—*"

The old man sat down heavily. "I know what became of your friend the priest," he told Richard. "They were talking about him; a very decent fellow as priests go, they said, not like some of the black crows. He had a stroke a week ago and was taken to the hospital. It seems he's not expected to recover. So it's as well you came out of that hole in the ground you told us about when you did."

"I'm sorry," said Richard. He was not altogether surprised for he had often felt very anxious about Don Luigi when he had come with provisions. He was always short of breath, and there had been ominous grey shadows about his mouth and in the hollows of his temples. "I'm terribly sorry. I hope it wasn't looking after me brought it on."

"Don't worry," said Pellico. "He did what he thought was right. He seems to have been that sort of man." There was a short silence. Pellico sat with his work-worn hands on his knees, leaning forward in an attitude eloquent of dejection and fatigue. Tonietta looked scared and the two young men gravely attentive. It was evident that there was more to come.

"They say some Germans are to be quartered here. They have taken over the Albergo Centrale. Some say the army, and some the SS men or the Gestapo. They say the district is to be combed out for volunteers to work in the Reich. The Reich. That means Germany, doesn't it? Volunteers," he said bitterly. "That won't be all, of course. They'll rake about for hidden stores of wine and oil and anything else that takes their fancy, and beat us up or shoot us if we dare to complain."

"When are they coming?" asked Aristide. "Did you hear that?"

"No one knows for certain, but it may be to-morrow." Aristide rubbed his ankle reflectively. "We'll have to get out of here, mate. Marching orders."

Tonietta burst out crying.

Aristide patted her on the back. "That's all right, ducks," he said, and then, "Cor! I'm always forgetting you don't understand English—"

"Accidente," grumbled his uncle, "they would come now, those animals, just when we want them least. I can't keep you here—but where can you go?"

"Why not the place where I was hiding?" said Richard. "We'd be safe enough there for a day or two anyway, if we could take a supply of food with us."

"Sicuro," said Aristide cheerfully. "Stop blubbing, Toni, you're making my shirt quite damp. What do you say, *zio?*"

Old Pellico was less sanguine, but there seemed to be no alternative. They would have to go during the night. The town gates would be closed, but he had a friend whose house was built up against the wall. It was possible to climb out of the attic window.

The wall was old and crumbling and there were plenty of foot-holds. In fact, it was a recognised route for persons who for one reason or another wanted to avoid the ill-bred curiosity of the *dogana* officials. Naturally his friend expected some compensation for his trouble.

Aristide, grinning, produced a note for fifty lire. "Will that be enough?"

His uncle took it from him. "Leave all that to me. You shall have all the food we can spare. You'll pay for it, won't you? I wouldn't rob my own nephew, but you were supplied with money by the English Government—or so you said when you came—"

"Quite right," said Aristide largely. "There's plenty more where that came from."

When Toni and her father had gone into the shop to collect provisions, he turned to Richard. "I admit the old boy has an eye to the main chance," he said defensively, "but you can't blame the poor old perisher. Look how they live here, eating muck we wouldn't give to the pigs, and Toni forever mending and patching their clothes."

"That's OK," said Richard. "They are taking big risks with us. I only wish I could pay my share. It's bad luck I lost my pocket book."

"You don't think they pinched it up at that farm?" Richard did not. He was sure the Donati were honest. Old Pellico and the girl were busy in the shop, working by the light of one candle, tying up two parcels of sausages and cheese and bread. Aristide joined them and Richard could hear the old man mumbling away with an occasional comment or exclamation from his nephew, but he could not follow what they were saying.

He was wondering if it would be possible to get into touch with Alda through Tonietta. If he wrote a letter could she deliver it?

It would not be safe to call at the Villa, but there might be some other way. He wanted to see her again. He wanted that more than anything.

No, he thought, to involve her any further would be the most damnably selfish thing he had ever done. After the war, if he lived, he would come back. Meanwhile, it was no time for love-lorn musing, for they were evidently going to be in a tight spot.

Aristide, coming in, found him shaving before the little cracked mirror on the wall.

"Dolling up? Got a date?" he enquired.

"There isn't much light where we're going."

Aristide grunted. "Well, we won't be there long, I hope. We'll lie low to-morrow, and that'll give this blasted ankle time to rest after to-night's beano, and then, after dark, if all's well, we'll get on with the job. Got to pick up the doings first. I can find the place all right. I got my map. And then we'll make for the coast."

"Will your ankle hold out?"

The little ex-waiter shrugged his narrow shoulders. "It'll damn well have to." He hesitated. "Of course it's my job, not yours. I mean, I was dropped here for the purpose, and you wouldn't be here at all if the plane hadn't crashed—"

"Rubbish," said Richard vigorously. "We're in this together. It means as much to me as to you. Unless"—it was his turn to look uncertain—"unless you think you'd get on better without me."

"Not me. If you're willing. I'm glad to have you." They were all rather silent at supper, a supper of bread and onions and scraps of salted tunny, washed down by the harsh red wine of the country. Old Pellico looked anxious, poor Toni's plump face was red and swollen with crying, and Aristide's cheerfulness was synthetic. Richard fancied that now and then they all looked rather oddly at him. He even wondered vaguely if they were keeping something from him, but he thought it best not to force the issue. Sooner or later, if there was anything more he must be told, he would hear it from Aristide.

Chapter X
CONVERSATION IN A TOMB

"Some tomb," said Aristide admiringly, as they ate their breakfast of bread and cherries some hours later, "fancy being done with the missis to sit on your own coffin like. Tasty, I call it. Reminds you of Madame Tussaud's in a way.

And those little pots and saucers were for their grub? How long since all this was fixed up, do you know?"

"Don Luigi said it might be about three thousand years."

"Cor blimey!" Aristide, much impressed, stared hard at the two semi-recumbent figures on the lid of their sarcophagus.

"They didn't give you the horrors when you were here alone?"

"No. They look harmless enough. Rather a stodgy bourgeois couple. How's your ankle?"

"Swollen up a bit," admitted Aristide, "but we got down that wall a treat, didn't we. And we can get in again the same way if we ever pay Mont Alvino another visit. We might, you know, a commando raid."

The rock-hewn underground chamber seemed pleasantly cool after the Pellico's kitchen. Richard had collected a heap of dry fern and dead leaves to make a bed when he was there before, and there was Don Luigi's blanket. The two fugitives had made themselves as comfortable as they could and lay on their backs watching the crack in the roof as they talked. When night had fallen they must be on their way.

"Will the tunnel be guarded?" asked Richard.

"I got within a hundred yards of the entrance that night. There was a lean-to hut just by the arch, and a couple of chaps watching the red glow in the sky from our burning plane."

"Was that why you didn't do the job then?"

"No. My instructions were to put in a bit of time in Mont Alvino first. They'd done a posh job with my papers after I told them about my uncle. I had the contacts, see. I was to find out if there was any underground resistance movement organised, and, if not, to see if anything could be started. You see, mate, Mont Alvino is a one-horse place that nobody's ever heard of, but it's only twelve miles from the sea as the crow flies—though more like twenty if you don't happen to be a crow. And it's on a branch line—but the Jerries might find it useful if the main lines get blocked."

"And did you find out anything—I mean about a resistance movement?"

"I asked *lo zio*. He'd have known if there was one. They're sick of il Duce and his bullies, they're sick of being pushed off to Spain or Africa, they're sick of all this blah about glory and the great Italian Empire, and they hate the Jerries; but that's all so far. And they don't really know what's happening. There aren't many wireless sets in the town and they can't get the B.B.C. because of the mountains being so near or something. They're an ignorant lot," said Aristide in pitying tones. "What are the orders for after the fireworks?"

"'Get out if I can—and that goes for you, too, of course. And a sub will look out for signals from La Folletta the night of the 15th and, failing that, the 20th."

"Where's La Folletta?"

"The nearest point on the coast. A small fishing village. We might make it—with luck."

"What's to-day?"

"The thirteenth."

They were both silent for a while.

Aristide moved restlessly and scratched the back of his neck.

"Curse these mosquitoes." He sighed. "Toni's a nice kid. When the war's over I'm going to fetch her. We'll open a little restaurant same as mum and dad did. Toni'll be a first-class cook. She didn't do too bad with that soup she made out of God knows what."

"She seems a good sort," said Richard. "I would have liked to have asked her to take a letter to the Signorina Olivieri, but I was afraid it might get her into trouble. You see—I don't know if you guessed—I hope to come back myself after the war and—and try my luck."

There was a perceptible pause. Richard had time to be sorry he had spoken, but it was too late now. Aristide moved uneasily.

"Well—but you don't really know her, mate," he argued, "seeing her a couple of times like that. It's just a fancy, like having a pin-up Hollywood cutie tacked on the wall over your bed. Why, a chap like you'll be able to pick and choose at home if you want to settle down after the scrap's over."

"Damn you, Pellico," said Richard furiously, "how dare you refer to Signorina Olivieri as a cutie. What the hell is it to do with you anyway?"

"Nothing. But I thought we were pals. Sorry I presumed. Of course I know you're a gentleman and all the rest of it, old school tie and all that muck, and I'm just a waiter, a bloke who runs about with a napkin over his arm getting flat feet and saying sir, and grovelling for a sixpenny tip."

Richard sat up. "For God's sake don't let's quarrel. I suppose you meant well. It's just that I happen to be in earnest. Let's drop the subject. Forget it."

"O.K.," said Aristide. "No hard feelings. Look, we ought to have a bit of shut eye."

"You're right."

They both settled down to sleep through the heat of the afternoon, and Aristide dropped off almost at once, but Richard lay awake for some time. He knew that the young Italian was becoming strongly attached to him. It was a mutual liking, for he had seen enough of Aristide to know that there were very sterling qualities underlying the apparently irresponsible Cockney good humour that made him such an engaging companion. He knew that he must acquit him of any intention to give offence. That being so what had he meant by saying what he had said about Alda? "I must get to the bottom of it," thought Richard, and soon after fell into a deep sleep.

When he woke it was dark and Aristide was opening out their parcel of provisions by the dim light of a carefully shaded candle.

"We'll halve what's left in case we get separated. Nice little nap you've had."

"Is it time to start?"

Aristide had a watch. He looked at it before he replied. "In about an hour from now."

They ate in silence. When they had finished the food that remained was divided as Aristide had suggested.

"I could do with a smoke," said Richard sighing.

"So could I." Aristide sat hugging his knees, his small, sallow face rather pale in the candlelight, his big dark eyes wistful.

"What couldn't I do to a plate of sausages and mash—"

"Aristide, what did you mean a while back about—about Signorina Olivieri?"

"I—I don't want to hurt you, mate."

"Good God! Has something happened to her? Don't sit there gaping at me, man. Out with it."

"It's something *lo zio* heard yesterday. He wouldn't say anything before you. I wouldn't have told you, but perhaps you'd better know. The fact is she's been arrested—" He seemed to find it difficult to go on.

Richard felt as he had sometimes felt in the plane when it dropped in an air-pocket. He jolted back into complete consciousness and found a voice that sounded not unlike his own.

"Because—because of me?"

"No. Nothing to do with you. At least—" Aristide hurried on. There was no need to dwell on the theme of the secret lover. "It's on account of what happened up at the Villa. The marchese Gualtieri's daughter-in-law was taken ill and died in the night. The doctor had been sent for and he said she was poisoned. Arsenic, it was. And the person that prepared the drink that the poison was in and gave it to her was her cousin."

"Ridiculous. Impossible. Alda was devoted to the marchesina. In any case—a poisoner. They must be mad."

"Don't take it so hard. Maybe there's some mistake. If she's innocent she'll be able to clear herself," said Aristide, but his tone lacked conviction.

"There's no if about it. But, of course, you don't know her. You've only to look at her—"

Aristide shook his head. "I don't want to hurt your feelings—but you can't be sure."

"What motive do they suggest?"

"Well, it's all rumour and hearsay, and what the servants overheard. All that's known for certain is that the police were sent for, that the prefetto and several of his men were there for several hours questioning everybody and searching the rooms, but the story is that the marchesina and the signorina quarrelled, that the marchesina had found out something about her cousin and threatened to tell tales." He hurried on, hoping that Richard would not grasp the significance of this point. "That wouldn't amount to much. My sisters often quarrelled, fought like cats they did at times, but it didn't mean a thing. If she didn't do it, she'll be out again in a few days."

Richard had been sitting with his head in his hands. He looked up now. "Is there anything I can do? Would it help her if I gave myself up? No, I suppose not."

"Maybe I shouldn't have come out with it all," said Aristide unhappily. "Only I thought if she's no good it's better you should know, see. Cut it out in time, see, and not go on kidding yourself—"

Richard made no reply, and after another pause Aristide looked at his watch again and said briskly: "Time we got going."

Richard got up at once, the candle was extinguished, and they crawled through the hole in the wall, replacing the old sacks that covered it, and through the screen of brambles and undergrowth into the open air.

CHAPTER XI
THE MARCHESE MAKES TWO CALLS

AFTER the funeral Silvio had driven the marchese and his lawyer back to Rome, dropping the latter at his villa in the Prati quarter on the way to the great gloomy Gualtieri palace in the Piazza Navona.

The marchese asked his young relative to dine with him that evening, but when Silvio excused himself on the ground of arrears of work he did not press the invitation. Silvio was understood to have some not very well defined secretarial post in one of the Ministries.

The marchese, who disliked and distrusted Fascism but was far too wary to say so, was careful never to enquire into

Silvio's political activities. A pack of *mascalzoni*, he thought distastefully, but it was convenient to know someone who could obtain a supply of petrol for his car and the necessary permits if he wanted to use it. It was a long and tedious cross-country journey by rail to Mont Alvino.

"You are not too tired, I hope," said Silvio as he lifted the marchese's suitcase out of the back of the car and gave it to the portière. With Gualtieri his manner was always quiet and deferential.

"No. No. You have been very helpful, Silvio. I shall not forget it. On second thoughts, you may drive me a little farther to the convent in the Via Due Macelli. My sister will wish to hear—"

Don Gaetano's only sister had taken the veil when she was twenty, when the man she was to have married, finding himself unable to pay his gambling debts, had shot himself in the bedroom of the dancer who had helped him spend his money. That was a long-forgotten scandal. Virginia Gualtieri had been forty years in the convent and was now the Mother Superior. She sat very quietly in the bare room where visitors were received, and listened to her brother's description of his daughter-in-law's death. She was very like him, with the fine-drawn austerity of a portrait by El Greco.

Long years of repression had turned her face into a delicately carved ivory mask in which only the smouldering black eyes were alive. Her hands were hidden in the long sleeves of her habit.

"Poor child," she said. "She came to see me once, when she and Amedeo were in Rome after their honeymoon. She was charming. A little foolish perhaps, but one forgives that in so pretty a creature. We will pray for her, all of us here.

We will pray. How anyone could have the heart—this cousin of hers—you had her to live at the Villa?"

"Yes. She is an orphan. The two girls were brought up together. They appeared devoted. Chiara clung to her."

"How old is she?"

"Eighteen, I believe."

"Madonna mia," murmured the nun. "Are they sure, Gaetano?"

"The evidence is overwhelming."

"Has she confessed?"

"No."

"You have seen her?"

"No. She had been taken to the prison."

"What do they say was the motive?"

"They think she had a lover, and that Chiara tried to put an end to the affair and threatened to tell Amalia Ferrucci."

"There is proof of that?"

"They are looking for proof."

"It might even be jealousy," said the nun thoughtfully. "She may have resented the care and attention lavished on Chiara. If she had been a year or two younger I should have been less surprised. There are difficult and sometimes dangerous moments during the passage from childhood to adolescence. Was she moody at times?"

"I'm afraid I cannot tell you. I hardly noticed her. Naturally they were quiet when I was present, but I used to hear them chattering and laughing together—not, of course, since Amedeo's death."

"Amalia Ferrucci has been in charge of the household since your wife's death. It is a responsible post. You have found her satisfactory?"

"Entirely. She has been invaluable. She nursed my poor Lucia devotedly through the last phases of her long illness. I do not know what I should have done without her during these three years. Chiara, of course, required a duenna during Amedeo's frequent absences, and she was far too young and inexperienced to manage the servants. She is"— the marchese spoke with unusual warmth—"a pearl among women."

His sister eyed him reflectively. "Should I like her?" He seemed struck by her question. He considered it before he shook his head. "I cannot say. Perhaps not. Would you like to make her acquaintance? She could come here next time she is in Rome."

"Are you thinking of marrying her?"

He did not take offence. Virginia had always been forthright.

"I have thought of it more than once just recently. There is my grandson to be thought of. He is still at the podere with his foster-mother. But presently he will be brought down to the Villa. I shall supervise his education myself."

For the moment he was almost animated. The nun watched him with affectionate understanding. He was looking forward ten, twelve years, teaching a boy to ride and shoot.

"I must consider it," he said. "While she was at the Villa as duenna to the two girls there could be no suggestion of impropriety. Her duties were well-defined. But now, if I spend much of my time there it will be different."

"It is a good place to grow up in," said the nun gently. "I was happy there as a child."

He smiled for the first time. "You climbed all the trees. You horrified your governesses. You should have been a boy, Virginia—" He checked himself.

"Will there be a trial?"

"I suppose so. If everything does not fall to pieces first."

"What do you mean?"

"Listen—"

"You mean the guns," she said placidly. "They sound nearer to-night. But they will not touch us here. Barbarians have come and gone. Rome remains."

"Rome, perhaps. But the rest of the country is not so fortunate. This comes of encouraging the bullfrog to bellow like the bull," growled her brother.

A bell rang somewhere in the convent. The Mother Superior glanced at the white-faced clock on the wall. "You must go now. Thank you for coming, Gaetano." She hesitated. "I wish I could advise you. There must be more in all this than has yet come to light. We will pray for you. We will beg the blessed Santa Chiara to intercede for her namesake, and the Holy Mother of God to watch over the little one, last of all the Gualtieri."

She stood with bowed head, and clasped hands hidden by the long sleeves of her habit, as her visitor went out. A lay sister was waiting in the corridor to take him across the *cortile* to the entrance where the portière unlocked the gate for him.

Gualtieri walked back to the Piazza Navona. Though the golden-brown walls of the houses were still exhaling the heat stored during the burning hours of noon, the little breeze that comes up from the sea at sunset was cooling the air, and it was pleasant to hear the splash of water in the fountains. There were many people in the streets, sitting on the church steps, wandering aimlessly.

Shabby people, harassed and hungry-looking, stepping back hurriedly into doorways when swaggering young men in the smart black Fascist uniform or the more heavily-built florid soldiers of the Reich clattered by. Rome was packed to suffocation with refugees from the north and the south. The marchese knew that all his tenants in the Palazzo Gualtieri were harbouring relations or sub-letting their rooms at fancy prices. As he climbed the great marble staircase to the *mezzanino* he heard babies crying, women screaming remarks from one window to another, and he thought longingly of the silence and seclusion of the Villa.

Would he be able to bear it though now that they were all gone, his wife, his son, his daughter-in-law?

He dined alone, frugally, waited on by his old manservant, who was his foster brother and an uncle of Marietta Donati, who was his grandson's wet nurse. He talked to him as he crumbled his bread and sipped his wine, telling him of the funeral.

"Did His Excellency go up to the podere?"

"Yes. They were all well there. Marietta has not heard from her husband lately, but she and her parents hope he may be home on leave soon. I shall leave the child with them until the autumn when Marietta will wean him. If the war is over then I shall get an English nurse for him."

"Why, Excellency?"

"They are hygienic, and they don't spoil the children and over indulge them as our women do."

Nicolo, who had never heard of hygiene, murmured that it must be as His Excellency pleased, and added philosophically that nothing mattered if it was true, as people were saying, that the world was coming to an end.

"The world we knew," said his master. "*Bene*, Nicolo. I shall not be wanting anything more."

"His Excellency will not be going out again?"

"Not to-night. I am tired."

He had thought he might visit Rosina, but the little horse-cabs were scarce and the wretched underfed animals that drew them were as likely as not to drop dead between the shafts going up the hill to the Ludovisi quarter; he detested the trams packed with unwashed, sweating humanity, and it was too far to walk after a long and fatiguing day. Rosina was as soft and comfortable as a child's woolly toy, a plaything for an elderly baby. To-morrow, perhaps.

He spent a part of the following morning with his lawyer. There were papers to be signed and various matters to be discussed in connection with Chiara's death. She had made no will, but a little money that had come to her through her mother would revert to Alda Olivieri.

"Can she profit," asked the marchese harshly, "from the death of her victim?"

"The matter must remain in abeyance for the present," said Bianchi.

He wondered if he should mention a rumour which he had heard through his clerk, that bombs had been dropped on Mont Alvino during the night. He decided to say nothing about it. It might not be true, and his client had quite enough on his mind already. The marchese looked very lean and very grey and desiccated in light of a summer morning. He had never really recovered from the shock of his only son's death. He must be induced now to concentrate his thoughts and his affections on his grandson and heir. Bianchi was glad to find that the child was already taking his place in his plans for the future. He seemed in better spirits when he left the lawyer's office. He lunched at his club, and after drowsing for an hour over a magazine in the club reading-room, he thought he would spend an hour or two with Rosina.

She had been living for the past two or three years in a small furnished flat he had taken for her. It was on the sixth floor of a modern block of apartments. The porter who knew him was not in the vestibule, but the lift was automatic. He got out at the sixth floor and rang Rosina's bell.

He waited, but she did not come. Usually he could hear her, the clacking of her high heels or the shuffling of the little pink velvet mules he had given her. She might be out and, in that case, he would use his key and let himself in and wait for her. There was a comfortable armchair dedicated to his use in the tiny, over-furnished *salotto* where the shutters were always carefully closed to keep out the light and the heat.

Rosina's flat always smelt rather like a hairdresser's shop with its mingled odours of violet powder, Soir de Paris, and curls singed by too hot an iron, on a foundation of coffee, fried onions and defective drains. As Gualtieri sat looking about him, prepared to be tolerantly amused by the litter of tattered novels, cherry stones and crumpled gloves and scarves, he noticed the complete absence of these accessories. The room was unnaturally tidy. Even the usual pile of music on the top of the piano had been cleared away. He got up, frowning a little, and went into the bedroom. Here no mistake was possible, the array of boxes and bottles, the brushes and scissors were gone from the dressing-table, and the nightdress case of rucked pink satin no longer lay on the bed. He jerked open the door of the wardrobe, pulled out the drawers of the chest. Rosina had left, taking with her all her possessions.

He found the letter eventually on the table in the tiny kitchen.

"Dear and Honoured Friend and Protector,

Try to believe that I am not ungrateful for all your kindness. I am sorry to leave you so abruptly, but I am called to join one who needs me. It is for me a great and proud destiny. I never dreamed that he had noticed me. My poor Bibi, I am afraid you may miss your Rosina at first, but I hope you may find another *piccola amica* who will be more worthy of you. I owe sixty lire to the grocer, and the larger of the two frying pans belongs to the tenant overhead. It should be returned to her or she will make a fuss. For the last time I sign myself,

YOUR ROSINA

The sprawling hand and the erratic spelling were familiar and the reminder about the borrowed frying pan was characteristic, but the marchese was puzzled by the mysterious reference to a great and proud destiny. "What is the little fool jabbering about?" he said aloud irritably. Rosina was no figure of romance. She had been pretty with a wax doll prettiness, but she was past her first youth and growing very stout. She might have been wanting to settle down and regularise her position. If some decent tradesman had wanted to marry her, he would not have stood in their way. He might even have settled something on her as a dowry.

He was more annoyed than hurt, she had never been much more to him than a pet animal, but he felt a certain sense of desolation as he glanced for the last time round the room where already the dust was lying in a fine film on the dressing-table and the mirror in which he had so often seen her laughing reflection as she sat brushing her hair. She had laughed easily and often, and he was old and sad. "She need not have left me like this," he thought as he went down again in the lift.

The *portière*, a greasy, slovenly fellow, his waistcoat unbuttoned over a soiled shirt, touched his cap to the marchese.

Gualtieri stopped to speak to him, disliking the necessity but willing to get it over.

"The signora has gone away. The rent is paid until the end of this month but you can let it as soon as you like. Here is the key. There is a frying pan belonging to a tenant on the seventh floor. See to it."

"Sicuro." The man looked as if he expected to be questioned, but Gualtieri, angry and humiliated, only wanted to get away.

The *portière*, looking after him, grinned and shrugged his shoulders. "Just as well perhaps," he mumbled. "After all the other paid me to keep my mouth shut."

CHAPTER XII
CONVERSATION ON A TERRACE

DONNA Amalia had dined alone in the little *salotto* and was drinking her coffee on the terrace when Silvio arrived.

She thought, as she had often thought before, how well the smartly-cut black riding breeches and the black shirt became his slim graceful figure.

"Back so soon?"

"Captain Haussmann and Major Weiss have been sent down from headquarters to investigate last night's affair. Did you feel it here?"

"The house shook. I thought it was an earthquake. But no windows were broken."

"You were lucky. There is hardly a pane left the other side of the town."

"What was it exactly? We hear nothing shut away here."

"Sabotage. The railway tunnel collapsed just as a troop train was entering. The engine and the three front carriages were buried under a mountain of earth and rubble and the back part of the train caught fire. Breakdown gangs and Red Cross people are busy at the other end of the tunnel. Nothing can be done from this end. Mont Alvino is sealed off from the north. The Nazis are furious. This little branch line might have been very useful. They blame us for not guarding it more efficiently. But there seemed no danger. There were always two men on duty at the tunnel's mouth to prevent any unauthorised person going in, and it couldn't be got at from the air."

"What have they to say?"

"The guards? They have not been found. Blown to pieces probably. Anyhow our German friends are out to make as many people as possible wish they'd never been born. If they don't find something it won't be for want of trying."

"But why are you here?"

"I am acting as a guide and interpreter."

"Couldn't you have got out of it?"

"Why should I?"

"It will make you unpopular with the people here."

"Does that matter?" he asked, smiling.

"You have not forgotten that if all goes well you may inherit this property?"

"No. But you don't imagine I should live in this hole. Never mind that. One thing at a time. One must seize one's opportunities. I will tell you something that will make you laugh."

"Tell me then, *caro*," she said fondly.

He sat on the balustrade, looking down at her, lithe and active as a black cat, his cold greenish-blue eyes alight with amusement.

"I went to call on the fair and frail Rosina."

"Silvio—"

"I had left him at the convent where he had gone to get sympathy, I suppose, from his sister. I felt tolerably sure we shouldn't meet. If he had come while I was there I could have hidden in a cupboard."

"But I thought you said she was so discreet and well conducted—" began Amalia.

"Wait until you hear. She seemed surprised to see me, and she did not ask me in at first. I told her I was the bearer of a message from a personage of the first importance. She merely gaped at me. She is very stupid. I asked her if she had ever seen the Duce close to. She said twice, the first time at a parade of the balilla when she had a seat in the stand just facing the stage where he stood to give away prizes, and the next time at the Teatro Nazionale when she happened to be in the corridor on her way to the ladies' room just as he was coming out of his box with his party. She said he looked at her. Obviously the little idiot had been tremendously flattered by the great man's notice. I had reckoned on something of the sort. Ciano would have done as well, or even—I said, that in that case what I had to say would no come as a complete surprise. I lowered my voice mysteriously, and she invited me in.

"By this time she was twittering with excitement and ready to swallow anything. I told her that I would mention no names, but that a certain person was profoundly *inamorato*. There had been many women in his life, but the sentiments she had inspired were without parallel in his experience—I can't remember everything I said—a lot of blah—but she loved it—her fat face was quivering with emotion. I came to the point. If she was willing to join him she must travel north that same night. I would see her on to the train for Verona where all arrangements would be made for her comfort and convenience, and he would come to her when he could snatch a few hours of freedom from the tremendous burden of his responsibilities. I gave her half an hour to pack. Actually she was ready in forty minutes. She wrote a farewell letter to the marchese and let me read it. It was very nice. I wonder what he made of it. I fetched a cab and took her to the station. It was dark by that time, and she was very confused and left everything to me."

"But, Silvio, she'll come back from Verona when she finds she has been tricked, and complain to—no, she would hardly have the courage to complain to Gualtieri after letting him down. All the same she might be dangerous to you—"

"She was not going to Verona. The train I put her or was taking volunteers' to work in Germany. She won't come back."

"I see," she said. She was not shocked, but sometimes her son's devilish ingenuity startled her. She was proud of her own capacity for intrigue, but he was always a step ahead of her.

"That leaves your way open. You ought to pull it off easily now," he said.

"Yes. I think I shall." She sounded confident. They sat for a while quietly enjoying the cooler air. Fireflies glittered like greenish diamonds in the rosebushes at the foot of the terrace. Behind them the great house loomed dark against the starlit sky.

Silvio lit a cigarette. He always had his case well filled, just as he always had plenty of petrol. "When will the girl be tried?"

"I do not know. The prefetto came to see me this morning. He was very civil. He told me that she is being questioned. She denies everything. They are convinced that she has been meeting some man. She used to go into the town with Caterina, and go to confession and hear mass while the old woman was at the market buying the provisions. That at least was her excuse."

Silvio grinned. "You didn't look after her particularly well, did you?"

"I thought if she got herself into a mess it would be as good a way as any of getting rid of her."

"Do you know who the man was?"

"I have no idea. They have questioned the sacristan at the Duomo and some of the old women who attend the services every morning. They knew Alda by sight, but they say she was always alone. She seemed very friendly with the old priest who was her confessor, they were often talking together, but he had a stroke a week or two ago and has since died in the hospital. He lived with his niece, a young war widow, and she used to come here to do sewing. We had her quite recently. She turned that black silk coat for me. She was very clever and ' quite cheap. A mousy little thing. That type is often sly. She may easily have acted as a go-between, though I doubt if she would have done much without payment, and Alda had no money. They might have got something from her, but she had left the town, she went directly after her uncle's funeral, and no one seems to know when she has gone."

"It might be just as well if the man is not found, so long as the police remain convinced of his existence," said Silvio thoughtfully.

"It is not in my hands."

"Just between ourselves—did you invent him?"

"No. I am sure there was someone. I noticed a change in her. The girl was in love. One can always tell. She was more alive. She was excited. I have tried to get something out of Caterina, and the prefetto went all over it with her this morning. She is up and about again though her arm is still swollen. You know what these peasants are when they don't choose to speak. She pretends to be deaf, blind, and half-witted."

"She would soon snap out of that if the prefetto used modern methods," said Silvio, "if she were a political prisoner. We don't stand any nonsense." He looked at the luminous dial of his wrist watch. "I must be going."

"I still think you would be wiser not to be seen about too much with your German friends here." She hesitated, "You are quite certain you have chosen the winning side?"

"Of course," he said loudly and angrily, as if to silence some inner doubt. "Still—there is something in what you say. I tell you what—I will leave my car here in the garage. I can tell them it broke down. If I accompany them in one of their cars I shall not be noticed so much as if I was driving my own. I'll run it into the garage now and walk back to the town. Don't be alarmed if you hear shots during the next few days. This won't be the first purge Haussmann and the lieutenant have carried out. They are very efficient."

"I'll walk with you down to the gate when you have put the car away."

She took his arm as they went down the avenue. "Take care of yourself, *caro mio*."

He pressed her hand against his side. He and his mother had always been allies, she was the only human being for whom he had ever felt a spark of affection. "You'll be la marchesa here before long," he said, "you'll twist that old fool round your little finger as you always have done. We have not done so badly in the last two or three years, eh?"

They both laughed, and he kissed her and swung off, walking away briskly in the darkness while she returned to the house.

Chapter XIII
REFLECTIONS IN A DISTORTING MIRROR

For a while Alda had felt that everything she had known was slipping away from her, and that she herself was being carried along like a drowning creature drifting on a strong current. Desperately she caught at the grass growing on the banks, at overhanging branches, only to realise dimly that she was clutching at bedclothes, or at a hand that forced her gently but ruthlessly back.

"Lie still, my child, lie still—"

And then while she still cried for help there would be a sharp prick on her arm, and after that her screams died away and she slept.

Her world had changed utterly. The Villa and the woods were gone and in their place there was a whitewashed wall on which the shadows of three crosses fell at certain hours of the day. She wanted to ask if it was from twelve to three, but there was no one to tell her.

She heard voices, but was never sure if her own was one of them, and that terrified her because of the secret that must be kept. Richard. A name that must never be uttered, not even when the walls shook with a deafening roar and a shattering of glass and the lights went out.

Someone held her hand. Someone said: "It was a bomb, but the building is not damaged. Only a few windows broken. Don't be frightened, *figlia mia*."

Someone brought an oil lamp. She opened her eyes and saw a nun kneeling by her bedside. She said weakly: "Have I been ill?"

"Yes. Go to sleep now."

Gradually, it might have been the day after, her mind cleared and she remembered everything and realised that she was in the prison infirmary. They took her temperature and her pulse. She was better, and they knew it. She could not conceal the fact that she was hungry.

She ate the stew they brought her and drank a glass of wine.

The nun brushed her hair, buttoned her coarse cotton bed-jacket up to her throat and propped her up with pillows. She had been kind, but now her thin face was remote and unsmiling and she avoided catching Alda's eye. The girl's heart sank. Something unpleasant was going to happen.

The nun went out to the group of men waiting in the passage.

"She is ready for you now."

Doctor Sartini was small, plump, and swarthy. He had attended the Gualtieri family, but only for minor ailments until the night when old Pietro had fetched him and he had arrived just in time to see Chiara die. He stood in considerable awe of Donna Amalia Marucci, but she had been very gracious to him and though she had been shocked and horrified when he told her he suspected arsenical poisoning, she had not been obstructive. He had not been surprised when Alda had collapsed on her way to prison after her arrest. She had been dazed from the moment they woke her, and he suspected her of having taken a strong dose of some sedative before she lay down on her bed. He had been assiduous in his attendance while she lay semi-conscious in the infirmary. It was his duty, for he was the prison doctor, but, apart from that, he took a romantic interest in her case. It was not that he regarded her as the victim of a conspiracy. On the contrary, he was convinced of her guilt. He could hardly be otherwise since he had been standing by when the prefetto, searching her room, had found the half-filled packet of powdered arsenic under the handkerchiefs, in her sachet, at the back of a drawer filled with her scarves and ribbons.

So young and fragile looking, but—evidently—*une grande amoureuse*.

There were women who would go to any lengths, commit any crime, for love. He had read about them but never seen one before, much less held her thin small-boned wrist between his finger and thumb. It was, he told himself, like counting the heart beats of a tigress. He often felt sorry for her, but that did not prevent him from enjoying his part in the drama.

The prefetto, a much older man, had a more prosaic and drab point of view. The Gualtieri were an old family who had owned land and had a town house and a country estate in the province of Mont Alvino since the thirteenth century. There had been tragedies in those far off days when the *nobili* were a law unto themselves, it was lamentable that scandals should occur now when the local authorities were bound to intervene. The prefetto's sympathies were with the marchese who had had trouble enough in the last three years. He felt nothing but horror for Alda Olivieri, who had repaid her patron's kindness and hospitality by murdering his son's wife.

His assistant, a meagre little man with a straggling moustache and weak eyes, blinking nervously behind shell-rimmed spectacles, brought forward chairs while the doctor felt his patient's pulse.

"*Si. Si.* Much steadier. You may proceed—"

There were only three men but they seemed more. Alda felt surrounded, hemmed in. Their boots creaked, they had brought in with them into the clean bare room a faint stench that hung about dark uniforms worn too long in the heat of summer, stale sweat and tobacco, sour wine and garlic. She closed her eyes for a moment and called for help to some power outside herself.

The prefetto cleared his throat. "It will be better for you in the end if you are frank with us, signorina. You are very young. That will be borne in mind. We are inclined to believe that you have been led astray by a person who gained an influence over you. We know that you administered a fatal dose of arsenic to your cousin in the lemonade you prepared for her."

"No. I made the lemonade, but it was not poisoned. I never dreamed of such a thing. I loved Chiara."

As she spoke her eyes filled with tears. She fumbled under her pillow for her handkerchief.

"It is merely childish to deny what has been proved beyond any possibility of doubt," said the prefetto didactically. "You had a violent quarrel with her earlier that day."

"No. We never quarrelled. There was nothing to quarrel about. And Chiara was very sweet tempered."

"Very well. We will put it differently. You had a secret. You were meeting and corresponding with a man. The marchesina warned you that if you did not break off the connection she would have to inform Donna Amalia Marucci and the marchese. She gave you until the next day to think it over. You took advantage of those few hours to silence her."

"No."

"Donna Amalia overheard a few words of your conversation. It was not enough, unfortunately, to put her on her guard, but she remembered it afterwards."

"Donna Amalia is a liar."

"You are ungrateful, signorina. Donna Amalia has been most reluctant to make any admissions that could be used against you. She has been and still is greatly distressed. Everything that could be said for you has been said by her."

The prefetto's sallow face was flushed. He was really indignant. His voice, when he framed his next question, was perceptibly harder.

"During that day did you, for any reason, open the linen chest?"

She thought a moment. "Yes. I came in late for lunch. I was very hot and tired, and I thought I would have a bathe and change my dress. I went to the chest to get a bath towel."

"You knew that Caterina would be getting out fresh towels for all the rooms later in the afternoon? That was a part of the routine of the household."

"Yes. But I wanted my towel then."

"You took a towel—and you left a scorpion, didn't you?"

"I? You must be mad—"

"It was as good a way as any other of getting the cook out of the way for a few hours. Actually that was what happened. The scorpion stung her on the arm. The doctor here was sent for and she was put to bed. Normally she would have prepared the marchesina's lemonade."

"How did I get hold of a scorpion? Did I carry it about with me in my bag like a lipstick, or in a box? It's ridiculous. I'm afraid of them."

The prefetto slowly shook his head. "You say so, but there is more in you than meets the eye, signorina. You spend much time alone in the woods. That is unusual. You have been allowed to run wild. Donna Amalia blames herself for that, though she admits there was not much she could do about it. She was responsible for the young marchesina, not for you, and you could and did defy her well-meant advice."

"Is that what she says? I went two or three afternoons a week to visit Chiara's baby and his foster-mother. There is only one way to the Donati's farm and that is through the woods. The Donatis are charcoal burners, the farm is nothing really, a few goats and chickens and a patch of maize. Chiara could not go because of her heart so I went instead. It's rather a steep climb. Marietta brought the baby down to the Villa twice, but Chiara was so upset when the time came to take him away again that Donna Amalia said she must wait until he was weaned."

She stopped, panting a little. She was still very weak and inclined to tremble when she got excited. Besides, what was the use? He was not even listening. He went on as if she had not spoken.

"Your spiritual director was Don Luigi Cappelli. Formerly you went to confession once a month, but lately you have confessed every week, and you have been noticed on other occasions in the Duomo talking to this same priest. Don Luigi was an old man, and a man of unblemished reputation. On the other hand he was of humble origin and made no pretensions to wit or learning. What precisely did you find to talk about, signorina? I am not referring to what passed between you in the confessional naturally."

It was an awkward question. Alda answered it with a promptness that surprised herself.

"I have had some idea of becoming a nun. We talked about that."

"Was he persuading you?"

"No. He wanted me to wait and be quite sure I had a vocation."

"I suppose you told him that you were dissatisfied with the life you led at the Villa, that your cousin had everything and you nothing, that you had to wear her cast-off clothes and run her errands, and do the work of a maid without a maid's wages. You have always envied her, haven't you? You really hated her, though I don't suppose you told him that."

She stared at him. "It's like seeing yourself in one of those crooked mirrors they have at fairs. I didn't hate her. That's a lie. I loved her. There's a grain of truth in the rest of it. I wasn't happy at the Villa, but not because I envied Chiara. Since Amedeo was lost on patrol she's been so lonely and miserable. She clung to me. Oh, I hope they are together now. They are well out of this cruel world. So cruel and so stupid!" she said passionately.

What an actress! What fire! thought the little doctor admiringly. She's magnificent. But her outburst had done her no good with the prefetto.

"I suggest that you never had any intention of taking the veil. I suggest that you persuaded this simple-minded and unworldly old priest to act as a go-between in your clandestine love affair, and that the widowed niece who lived with him was also involved. You visited her at least once at their apartment, which was in a rough working-class quarter of the town, where normally a well-brought-up young lady would never dream of venturing alone."

"I went there once to ask if there was anything we could do after seeing Don Luigi in hospital. I was fond of him. Has he died since?"

"Yes. And his niece has disappeared. I daresay we shall be able to find her. We are taking steps."

Alda said nothing. She thought, if they find Filomena she will tell them everything she knows. Richard's life hangs on a thread. She saw Filomena at the Villa, a little, flat-chested, insignificant figure leaning over the table cutting into a piece of black silk with her big dressmaker's scissors. The Fate with the shears. Richard was not in uniform. They would shoot him as a spy.

The doctor, watching her face, said in a low voice: "She can't stand much more."

The prefetto grunted. So far the questioning had brought no new facts to light. A number of witnesses had been examined, the sacristan of the Duomo, old women who spent most of their time in the church, stall-holders in the market-place, and not one had seen her with any man other than the old priest who was locally regarded as almost a saint. Perhaps, he reflected, Donna Amalia had been wrong and there had been no clandestine love affair. But in that case what had been the meaning of the marchesina's threat to reveal her cousin's secret to her duenna and her father-in-law?

He decided to make an experiment.

"Very well," he said harshly. He leaned forward, keeping his eyes fixed on hers. "You won't speak. It does not matter. We have got your lover."

They all saw a shade like an impalpable grey veil pass over her face. The little brown head slipped sideways on the pillow.

"Per Dio!" cried the doctor angrily. "You have killed her!"

"Macche," said the prefetto with an unfeeling chuckle. "She's only fainted. Come," he beckoned to his subordinate, "we'll leave Sartini to bring her round. She's given herself away. There's a man somewhere in her background right enough, and we shall find him."

Chapter XIV
CARMELA'S BIRTHDAY PRESENT

THE man and woman lying on the lid of their terracotta tomb gazed blandly at their uninvited guest. Their smooth plump unwrinkled faces seemed to indicate that their lives had been quiet and uneventful. In any case their ashes had been undisturbed for three thousand years. Inside the sarcophagus the man's gold seal ring and the gold fibula with the snake's head that had fastened his cloak, and his wife's long gold ear-rings and her necklace of coral and lapis lazuli and cornelian beads still lay untouched on the grey film of dust and charred bone.

Richard had been asleep. He sat up, drank some water, and chewed mechanically at his last piece of dry bread, rubbing the green mould that covered it off on his ragged sleeve.

He was alone.

He had helped Aristide to knock out the two guards lounging outside their hut at the mouth of the tunnel. That had been easy. They were playing cards by the light of a shaded lanthorn and never knew what hit them. Aristide and Richard had dragged them off the line and left them in a ditch.

"If they'd been Jerries," said Aristide, "I'd have finished them off."

He was fey that night, his black eyes very bright. He had found what he called the doings, which had been dropped with him by parachute, where he had buried them, and he had insisted on going into the tunnel alone.

"I can do what has to be done. I don't need you, see. I want to do it," he said feverishly, "for Mum and Dad and the others, and especially for Carmela. To-morrow's her birthday, see. She'd have been eleven. I'm going to give her a trainload of Jerries for a birthday present."

"Don't go in too far. Allow yourself time to get out again," said Richard anxiously.

"Youbetcha. Once it's all set I'll run like hell. Three minutes they told me. Maybe a bit more. Now you be up there on the hillside, mate, where the earth is soft, and cover your head and you'll be O.K. I'll join you if I can and we'll make for the coast—but if, for any reason, we get separated, you just carry on, see. We've halved the grub and the money."

"Good luck," said Richard and held out his hand.

Aristide grinned. "We'll remember this and it'll seem like a dream when me and Toni have started our restaurant back of good old Leicester Square, and you come to dinner. Fancy me in a chef's cap and Toni at the desk—"

He gripped Richard's hand hard, and turned and vanished into the black mouth of the tunnel.

Richard climbed a little way up the hillside among gnarled olive trees, silvery grey in the faint starlight, and lay down where he could see Aristide come out again. His mouth was dry and his heart thumped against his ribs. How long was the tunnel? Half a mile?

Peering in, they had not been able to see the end of it. He knew very little about explosives. That sort of thing had never been his job. He fancied that Aristide knew very little more than he did. He had been chosen on account of his local contacts and because he could pass anywhere as an Italian. "If only he doesn't muff it," he thought with growing uneasiness as the minutes crawled by. "Come along," he urged, "buck up. Get a move on—"

He was straining his eyes watching the track. At any moment now Aristide should appear, running for his life, scrambling up the bank, away from the railway lines that gleamed like thin streaks of saliva flowing from a dragon's gaping jaws. "Buck up, for God's sake—"

There was a crash and a roar and the earth shook. Richard was blinded and deafened. There was a jarring pain in one. of his knees. After a while he staggered to his feet. He had been on all fours for a while, spitting out earth, and then he had been sick. He saw everything dimly through a mist, but it was not mist but dust which was slowly settling down again. The mouth of the tunnel was closed by a sloping mass of rubble like the stone screes at the foot of a mountain. The night was very still again, but the silence was broken by the wail of a siren in the town of Mont Alvino.

That meant that they would be coming soon to find out what had happened, the soldiers, the civil authorities. Richard knew that he must go. He could feel a warm trickle of blood running down his leg from where he had been hit by a flying bit of rubble.

If Aristide had got out he would have gone with him, trying to reach the coast. As it was he could do what he liked.

He turned back, and an hour later he was crawling through the screen of undergrowth into the old hiding place.

With care his food would last for a couple of days. As the after-effects of blast wore off he began to realise how unlikely it was that he would be free much longer. He was more alone than he had ever been. He could not endanger the Pellicos by going back to them, Don Luigi was dead, and Alda—what had happened to Alda was incredible. A nightmare. As long as he remained in the tomb he was probably safe, but the sabotage of the tunnel must have aroused even the easy-going local authorities, the woods would be searched, the guards at the town gates doubled. He would be taken within a few hours of leaving his sanctuary. After that the best he could hope for was that he would be shot without any preliminary beastliness.

He slept, and when he woke his spirits had risen a little. His luck might hold. The cut on his knee was not serious and was healing well. The singing in his ears was passing off. During the night he bathed in the little stream and refilled his jars with the cool spring water. During the day that followed he studied his map and tried to decide on his best course. He tried to keep his mind occupied.

He missed Aristide's cheerful chatter. He thought: "Damn it, why did I listen to him. I should have followed him into the tunnel. Then it would all be over."

CHAPTER XV
CONVERSATION IN A LIBRARY

COUNT Mario Cavagnin, a stranger in Rome, had lost his way in the maze of narrow streets between the Piazza Colonna and the Piazza Navona. When he emerged at last and saw before him the great fountains with their river gods and tritons and, wedged between palaces, the façade of the church built, according to the ancient tradition, over the foundations of the brothel where Saint Agnes' martyrdom began, he was hot and tired. He disliked being jostled by crowds, and the Roman cobbles hurt his feet.

He had set out reluctantly, urged on by his wife, to perform a disagreeable duty.

A hunchback beggar sitting by the church door, stopped whining for alms to point out the Gualtieri palace. Cavagnin dropped a small coin in the dirt encrusted palm, and entered the shady cortile. He was not surprised to see that the vast building had been let to so many tenants that it had taken on the dingy air of a tenement. He walked up the short flight of marble stairs to the mezzanino floor. A visiting card pinned to the door on the left of the landing indicated that the marchese had reserved this suite of rooms for his own use.

Cavagnin rang the bell and waited, sighing, and wishing himself anywhere else. Elena was right, of course, but he looked forward with dread to an unpleasant interview with poor Amedeo's father.

An elderly grey-haired manservant wearing a striped apron and list slippers took his card and asked him to wait while he ascertained if his master could receive him. He came back after a very brief interval and showed him into a dim shadowy room with book lined walls.

"Il signor Conte Mario Cavagnin, Eccelenze—"

The marchese, who had been seated at his writing table, rose and came forward to receive his visitor.

"You are, I think, a friend of my son's. I have heard him mention your name."

The marchese towered over the younger man, who was a little below the average height and slight in build. Cavagnin looked up at the lean, grave, bearded face.

"I cannot claim friendship," he said frankly. "My wife and I were on our honeymoon, and we happened to be staying in the same hotel as your son and his bride. We drank our coffee together on the terrace, and we went for some excursions together. We never met again. Our home is—or was—in Venice—but—you know how things are. We have come down to Rome to stay with relatives."

"Won't you sit down?" The marchese indicated a chair and sat down again himself. "Perhaps you did not know that my son was in the Air Force. He was posted missing."

"I had heard that. I am very sorry. He was charming. So young and so gay."

The marchese said nothing. He was sitting with his back to the light and Cavagnin could not see his face very well. He was very nervous and unhappily aware that he was being tactless.

He said: "I got mine in Africa over a year ago. My left arm. I'm just beginning to get used to the dummy. But I haven't come here to talk about myself. I—we read an account of the marchesina's death in the paper. Elena was horrified—and so was I, of course. She was so—*era tanta carina*—"

"*Diamine!*" he thought, "I must seem an interfering pushful person, intruding on his grief. If only Elena had come with me. She would have known what to say."

He sat staring in acute embarrassment at the erect and motionless figure facing him in the great carved chair. The marchese, meanwhile, was remembering what his son had said of the young couple he and Chiara had met at Como. Pleasant, well-mannered, not belonging to the new rich class or aggressive adherents of the Fascist Party, the husband a member of an old Venetian family, the wife a Manara of Turin. He could even recall what Amedeo thought of the little contessa. "A plain little thing, shrewd, sensible, and kind-hearted. Cavagnin obviously adores her, and does not mind in the least that she is cleverer than he is." No doubt, he thought wearily, this visit of condolence was well meant.

"It was good of you to come," he said stiffly. "I hope the contessa is in good health."

"Oh, quite," said Cavagnin. He cleared his throat. "I came for a reason. The fact is your daughter-in-law wrote to Elena about three weeks ago. She required some information. It was rather—well, Elena talked the matter over with me, and we decided that nothing we knew on the subject in question should be withheld. So Elena replied at some length. We know that the marchesina received her letter for she sent Elena a picture postcard with *Grazie Mille* written on it. Is all this news to you, marchese?"

Gualtieri looked steadily at his interlocutor. "I know nothing about it. Does this information concern Alda Olivieri?"

"No."

"Oh—" for a moment the marchese appeared disconcerted. "But you think it may be of some importance?"

"I am afraid so. Yes."

"Why afraid?"

"May I relate the facts? That would be the best way."

"Certainly."

"The marchesina wrote to ask if we knew anything of a certain Amalia Marucci who, until three or four years ago, had been living in Venice. She added that this person was related to your family and that she had been established for some time in your household where she held a responsible position as housekeeper and duenna to the marchesina. Elena brought the letter to me. Frankly—I was appalled."

He paused, but the marchese remained silent. Only one thing about him betrayed increased tension. The knuckles of the hands gripping the arms of his chair showed white under the wrinkled brown skin.

Cavagnin drew a silk handkerchief from his coat sleeve and wiped his forehead. "*Scusi.* What I have to say will be very disagreeable. I regret it. Amalia Marucci and her husband had run a gaming house in Venice. I was frequented by foreigners chiefly. Amalia also played the part of a discreet and obliging friend to young married women with elderly husbands. You know the sort of thing. Their house was convenient for assignations. It could be entered or left by three doors, each on a different canal. There were occasional scandals, but they were always hushed up. But after Marucci's death about eight years ago his widow found herself unable to carry on without him. She had to give up the house, and the furniture was sold to pay his debts. She disappeared for a time, to come back as one of those rather ambiguous figures dressed in shabby mourning who loiter in

the far corners of our churches, and beg for financial assistance in a genteel whisper if you let them get near enough.

"It's a chancy business, but la Marucci did very well at
it because she concentrated her attention on persons who
had good reason to fear her because of what she knew of
past indiscretions.

"She pushed her demands so far that in at least one case
her victim committed suicide. This is not hear-say. The
young woman in question was my uncle's second wife. She
drank sublimate, poor thing, but she lived long enough to
scribble a confession and an accusation.

"Again there was no publicity, our family could not face
the scandal, but la Marucci was warned that she must leave
Venice, and she disappeared again."

The marchese moistened lips that had gone dry before
he spoke.

"This is incredible. Donna Amalia nursed my late wife,
she has spent three years in my house, she has proven
herself worthy of my respect and my confidence. Never a
word—never a gesture—I cannot believe it," he repeated
half to himself. "There must be some mistake."

Cavagnin shook his head. "She had a son, a pretty fair
haired boy, a spoiled brat, spoiled and corrupt. I heard that
he was known to the Venetian underworld as the silver fish.
He was pointed out to me once in the Piazza San Marco.
He was pestering tourists, offering himself as a guide and
trying to sell dirty postcards. I have made some enquiries
here in the last day or two. I was told he had some sort of
post as a liaison officer with the Germans and is high in
favour with the Fascist Party." He hesitated and then said
bluntly: "Frankly, if I had known that, Elena might have left
your daughter-in-law's letter unanswered. I must ask you,

if you take any action, not to mention us by name. Though, of course, if they got hold of the letter they would know—"

"You are afraid of Silvio Marucci?"

"I am. And I'm not ashamed to say so. You know how things are just now in this unhappy country, with absolute power in the hands of a megalomaniac and his pack of canaglia."

"I agree," said the marchese curtly, "but this conversation is imprudent. You have said enough. I realise that my confidence was misplaced—this has been a shock. I have not yet faced all the implications—"

Cavagnin waited a moment. Then he said: "My wife and I made sure that the marchesina would lose no time in telling you what she had learned from us."

"There would have been time before—before her death?"

"Certainly. Even allowing for delays in the post."

"What made her think there was anything wrong? Did she tell you that?"

"Yes. She wrote that she detested her duenna and longed to get rid of her, but that unfortunately you had the utmost faith in her and let her have her own way in everything that concerned the household at the Villa. She added that Amedeo had disliked both her and her son and had always said he thought she had a past. She had learned from some chance remark of la Marucci that she had formerly lived in Venice, and it occurred to her that we might know something to her discredit."

The marchese sighed. "I am not very good at gaining the confidence of young people. Without intending it I overawe when I don't merely bore them. Most unfortunate in this case. I had no idea Chiara disliked Donna Amalia. Or—in fact it seems that I have been blind to many things that went on before my eyes."

"If you had known what you know now you would not have left la Marucci in charge?"

"Naturally not."

"If that letter fell into her hands—"

The marchese reflected. "She would destroy it, I imagine."

"Would that be enough? If the marchesina had read it—"

"Per Dio—" The marchese got up and walked about the room. "I see what you mean. Chiara—Chiara knew too much. A motive for murder. A woman without scruples, an intriguer. Then Alda—then that child is innocent. She has been used as a scapegoat."

"That is what we thought," Cavagnin agreed. "Elena and I have talked it over since we read an account of the affair in the paper. That is why we felt I must come to you."

"I am greatly obliged to you. But you made a stipulation just now. What can I do in this matter, signor conte, if you are not prepared to give evidence?"

Cavagnin shrugged his shoulders. "I see your difficulty. But you must see mine. Silvio Marucci won't take his mother's arrest lying down. If it became known that it was through me and my wife that her ugly past was brought to light, you know as well as I do what would happen. We are staying, as a matter of fact, with my wife's uncle in the Vatican City, where we should be fairly safe, but her mother, who is dying, has a flat in the Via Condotti, and Elena visits her every day, and we both have to come to my lawyer's office fairly often to go through formalities in connection with a transfer of land. On one of these occasions we should be surrounded by three or four black shirts, hustled into a waiting car, and—*addio*! Friends of mine have disappeared like that. The penal islands perhaps, but more likely the grave."

"'If—if she has found the letter your wife wrote to Chiara you are already in danger."

"I know it. I have taken what precautions I can. There is not much one can do. But my theory—and my hope—is that your daughter-in-law either destroyed the letter, or, more probably, hid it so well that la Marucci has not been able to find it, so that she only knows that somehow the marchesina learned the truth about her."

"Very well," said the marchese, "if I find that she has the letter there will be no point in further secrecy, but I promise that I will not be the first to mention your name. In any case, I am infinitely obliged to you. I am too late to save, but not to avenge."

Cavagnin had risen to take his leave. The marchese rang the bell and the old manservant came to show him out. The marchese went with him as far as the door of the library, uttering the civilities that his generation regarded as essential to polite intercourse.

Cavagnin could not but admire his iron self-control. But after the visitor had gone, Gualtieri walked back rather unsteadily to his chair by the fireless hearth, and called to Nicolo to bring him a little brandy. The old servant, noticing his greyish pallor, looked at him anxiously but dared not ask questions.

Gualtieri sipped the brandy and felt better, though the glass, as he set it down, shook in his hand. He had been numbed for a while, but now he was beginning to feel the full force of the blow to his pride and his confidence in his own judgment. That was bad enough, but there were other and more dreadful implications. This woman who, according to Cavagnin, was greedy, ruthless, without pity or mercy, and had harried one of her victims to her death, had nursed his wife through her last illness. Suppose she had hastened her end? It was not impossible. What had she to gain? The direction of his household power, and still more power.

After a while he unlocked a drawer in his bureau and slowly and thoughtfully went through its contents. A bundle of letters written by Chiara to her husband while he was in camp, framed photographs and snapshots he had pinned on the walls of his room in his billet, which had been sent to his father with his few possessions when all hope of his return had been abandoned. The marchese could not bring himself to read the letters. He knew that his son and Chiara had been lovers to the last. In that at any rate, he had not been deceived. But he studied the snapshots carefully. Most of them were of Chiara alone, sitting, standing, kneeling on the marble edge of the lily pond, the sun shining through her golden hair. But there were two of her evidently taken during their honeymoon in the hotel garden, with Count Cavagnin smiling down at her, and a young woman who was probably the Countess, on her other side, and there were several of a later date in which Alda Olivieri appeared.

In every case the two girls were obviously in high spirits, laughing, care-free, and on excellent terms with one another. In one picture they were arm in arm, in another Alda was sitting on the grass and Chiara was lying with her head on her cousin's lap.

He had heard the light girlish voices, the laughter, when he was reading or writing in the library at the Villa, voices hushed—if they remembered—as they approached his open window, for he was not to be disturbed. Chiara and her cousin, convent bred, had been well trained in the tradition of respect for the head of the family. At meals nobody spoke unless he addressed them. That rule was relaxed when Amedeo was at home. Chiara, encouraged by her husband's presence, had sometimes chattered freely enough, but he could not remember any utterance by Alda or that he had ever spoken to her beyond wishing her good night and good morning. He had not been interested. As a companion for his daughter-in-law she had seemed satisfactory, and that had sufficed. He had scarcely recovered from the shock of learning that she had committed a cold-blooded murder in an attempt to cover up her sexual depravity when he was asked to reverse his judgment and acquit her.

"She looks good," he muttered, "she looks charming."

She had been condemned unheard by him. When he reached the Villa she had already been taken away under arrest, and the evidence against her had seemed conclusive. Looking back he recalled Amalia Marucci's evident distress, the reluctance which she expressed to believe that Alda could be guilty. And he—he realised it now—had been blinded by his fury. She had played him as a matador plays a bull. She had been clever, damnably clever.

Slowly, but with hands that were quite steady now, he replaced the bundle of letters and the photographs and the few other odds and ends that had belonged to Amedeo in the drawer and relocked it. He kept out only one thing which he thought he might need before he had done what he had to do.

Chapter XVI
LAST WORDS IN A DRAWING-ROOM

THE prefetto had had his midday meal sent him from his usual restaurant. He felt disinclined to meet the other habitués of the Leon Bianco. They would not blame him, or, at any rate, not openly. It was not his fault that the guards on the line had not been numerous or vigilant enough to prevent sabotage. They would not mind about that. Not a few would rejoice that several hundred German soldiers had been lost in the landslide that buried the train that had just entered the tunnel a moment before the explosion. What mattered was that Mont Alvino was being held responsible. The Gestapo had arrived and were in control, functioning from the Albergo Centrale.

The prefetto sighed and swallowed a tablet. All this worry was affecting his digestion. He pushed his lunch tray to one side and rang his bell.

His room at the Questura was high-pitched, with frescoed walls and a magnificent carved ceiling, but the marble floor was grimy, and littered with torn paper and miscellaneous rubbish. The pigeon holes of his desk were overflowing with an accumulation of orders and counter orders, proclamations and warnings from headquarters.

The harassed secretary came in. "The Marchese Gualtieri to see you. I told him you were busy, but he says it is important."

"Show him in. And take this tray away. This meat is like leather—"

He rose to greet the marchese and the two men shook hands.

"Please sit down, marchese. What can I do for you?"

"It concerns the death—the murder of my daughter-in-law."

The windows were open and the shutters partly closed to keep out the heat and the glare. It was the hour of the *siesta* when the greater part of the population would be lying on their beds in darkened rooms. The prefetto suppressed a yawn. He usually took a nap himself about this time. But the marchese was a person of some local importance, who must be placated.

"Have no fear. Justice will be done. The prisoner is being examined daily. We shall induce her to speak before long. But, for the moment there are matters of immediate urgency which affect us all here. We are naturally very anxious." He cleared his throat. "As you are here, marchese, may I venture to hope that you will use your influence with your young relative to—to—in short"—said the prefetto, sweating freely—"mercy."

Gualtieri stared at him. "I do not understand you."

"*Madonna mia!* The Germans think the man or men who blew up the tunnel are hidden here. They have been searching every house. At intervals we hear shots. We do not even know if they shoot in the air to frighten people or if they shoot to kill. The officers have a car, and their men follow in a lorry. They have machine guns. To-day I hear they are combing the woods. There is a rumour that they will take hostages. And your—and Silvio Marucci is with them."

"I noticed that the streets were almost deserted," said Gualtieri. "I wondered—but I have nothing to do with politics. You know that, Menotti. I have held myself aloof. Rightly or wrongly. But my son wished it. He said that if I knew half of what was going on I should lose my temper—and then I should disappear—"

"One needs," said the prefetto, "a great deal of tact. Or influence. Just now, for instance. Naturally young Marucci will keep his German friends away from the Villa. You are fortunate, *caro signore marchese*, to have him as a member of your family."

Gualtieri seemed startled by this suggestion. "Really? Do you think I owe it to Silvio Marucci that I am not badgered by the canaglia who are running our country?"

Menotti reflected that in some ways the marchese was very simple and unsophisticated. That was what came of shutting oneself up in one's library and letting the world go by.

"Certainly," he said, "of course. But for him your Villa would almost certainly have been taken over as a hospital, or a home for war orphans, or perhaps merely a week-end retreat for the lady friend of some high personage. And probably the fact that he is related to you has meant that you have been spared the innumerable petty annoyances and restrictions that are our lot."

"I see," said Gualtieri slowly. "I have been blind to this as to other things. Can I be quite frank with you, Menotti? We have known one another all our lives. I believe you are an honest man."

Menotti shrugged his shoulders. "As honest as I can afford to be. I will be frank too. We are alone here. The system under which we have been living for over twenty years is corrupt, founded on lies, bombast, and blackmail. If I had been one hundred per cent honest I should have died years ago, or I should be living in exile, or rotting on one of the penal islands. I had a wife and three children— and I am not of the stuff of which martyrs are made. And so—I paid lip service to our heroic leader"—he flipped a finger at the large framed photograph of the Duce on his desk—"and here I am. *Eccomi.*"

"Those are politics," said Gualtieri. "But in the matter of the ten commandments, in the administration of justice?"

"As to that I think I can say that I do my best."

"Very well. I have something to tell you. It concerns Marucci and his mother."

He embarked on the story he had heard from Cavagnin, but without mentioning the name of his informant. Twice, while he listened, Menotti took out his handkerchief and wiped his face, but he made no comment until Gualtieri had finished. Then he said; "I have been favourably impressed by Signorina Olivieri. I have been finding it difficult to believe that she could be guilty of a cold-blooded and cruel murder. But—Donna Amalia—so gracious, so charming—so refined! It is incredible. I admit that her son is a *mascalzone*. Everyone knows that. But she—are you sure?"

"The person who told me is, I believe, reliable. And you can get corroboration from Venice. They must have been known to the police there."

"Probably," said Menotti. "But I told you just now, signore, that I have no taste for martyrdom."

Gualtieri was quite prepared to believe that. Menotti combined a fundamental good nature with his expressed determination to keep out of trouble. He could be trusted, but only up to a point.

Gualtieri thought a moment. "Do you mean that you are not prepared to take any steps that would lead to the arrest of Amalia Marucci for the murder of my daughter-in-law?"

Menotti looked nervously in the direction of the door.

"Hush, my dear friend, not so loud. I see that even now you do not realise the position. Listen to me. Silvio Marucci has no defined position, but he comes and goes as he pleases, there is always petrol for his car, and he smokes incessantly when, for the rest of us, cigarettes are not to be had. He is almost certainly a member of the OVRA, the secret police. I represent the municipal authorities with the Podesta, but I can assure you that we know very little more than the general public about these gentry. What we do know is that their powers are unlimited—almost—they are only responsible to headquarters. They tamper with private correspondence. It is a mere chance that those letters that passed between the marchesina and her Venetian friends were not read before they reached their destination.

"Any fresh move I made in this case would almost certainly be reported to Marucci, and if he saw—as he would see—that we had reason to suspect his mother he would act at once. Alda Olivieri would be removed from this prison to some unknown destination, and you and I would disappear. The vanishing trick. The OVRA are very expert. They have had a great deal of practice."

"God help us," muttered Gualtieri. He was convinced at last, in spite of himself. "Then is there nothing we can do?"

"We can play for time. The trial will not be yet unless Marucci pulls a good many strings, and he will not do that unless he thinks it necessary. We can keep her in the infirmary where she will be safer than she would be outside. The nuns are excellent women, and Doctor Sartini is my friend."

"You will do that much? I thank you." The marchese got up rather stiffly from his chair. He was upright as ever, but he looked older. The plump little prefetto glanced up at him anxiously.

"Discretion," he murmured, "the utmost discretion."

He saw the shadow of a smile pass over the lean, bearded face, like a gleam of wintry sunshine over the frozen surface of deep water.

"Have no fear," said Gualtieri. "I understand."

"Where—where are you going now?"

"To the Duomo. I will rest there for a while and meditate—in the presence of my dead."

The old sacristan roused himself from his afternoon doze to shuffle forward and unlock the wrought-iron gate of the Gualtieri chapel for the marchese. Gualtieri, who had known him for years, said: "How are you, Jacopo?" The old man did not answer him. Instead he touched his sleeve, a humble propitiating gesture, and said: "Eccelenza, you won't let them take hostages?"

Gualtieri felt sick. Here was another proof, if proof were needed, that he was associated in the public mind, with Silvio Marucci.

He said, with more harshness than he intended, "I can do nothing. Nothing." And the sacristan shrank away.

He stayed for a while in the chapel, kneeling on the dusty purple cushion on his faldstool, and staring vacantly at the picture of the Deposition from the Cross hanging over the altar, a dark and threatening work by Caravaggio. He was trying to think, but he could only feel, and remember. The pale, gentle face of his dying wife, smiling trustfully at her nurse, the voice of his son Amedeo saying, "If I don't come back from one of these flights you will take care of Chiara." The tiny, crumpled, red face of his grandson nuzzling the breast of his peasant foster-mother. The Donati were faithful, the child would be safe with them—but for how long?

That picture. His wife had always disliked it. It was the work of a master, but it was tainted by the moral degradation of the painter. It had no spiritual meaning. It was nothing more than the disposal of a corpse after a murder, the ugly aftermath of cruelty.

He shut his eyes and attempted to pray. No use. His contained fury must find a vent. He got up and went out, forgetting to bow to the High Altar or to dip his fingers in the stoup of holy water at the door.

There were two cabs on the rank in the piazza, aged, shabby vehicles with bony horses drooping between the shafts. Gualtieri got into one, and was driven out to the Villa half a mile beyond the town gate. He stopped the driver as he was about to turn up the avenue and got out and paid him.

"I could put you down at the door, Eccelenza."

"No. I will finish my journey on foot."

He walked slowly up the dusty private road between the acacias that had been in flower, scenting the air three weeks ago. Chiara had spoken of them in her last letter to him. Delicious at night, she had said, when we are sitting on the terrace. Perhaps in time she would have recovered from the shock of Amedeo's death and have regained her health and lived another fifty years.

The great house loomed up before him, looking almost as if it might be uninhabited, with its long rows of shuttered windows and its smokeless chimney stack but when he rang the bell Pietro came to the door, faltering at the unexpected sight of his master, with dust on his shoes and leaning heavily on his stick.

"Padrone—"

Gualtieri said quickly: "What servants remain?"

"Only me and Caterina. But—"

"Very well. Go into the kitchen and stay there until I fetch you. Do you understand. If the bell rings pay no attention. Donna Amalia is here?"

"*Si*, padrone. She has been resting in her room, I heard her come down a few minutes ago."

"What does she do with herself now that she is alone?"

"She has been occupied in turning out the drawers and cupboards in the rooms of the marchesina and of Signorina Alda."

"Very well. Do what I tell you now. Remain in your own quarters."

He found Amalia Marucci in the little *salotto* where Chiara had often sat with her cousin. She was standing by the open french window looking out across the terrace.

She was startled, but not disagreeably. Her first thought was that it was a good thing she had not begun the search she meant to make through the drawers and pigeon holes of Chiara's little carved and gilded bureau. It would not have looked well. She reflected with amused contempt and considerable satisfaction that it had not taken the great baby long to come crying to her to be comforted for the loss of his plaything. Silvio had been right after all when he got rid of the Rosina person. She told herself, with a thrill of triumph, that he would ask her to marry him before he left that room.

"Dear friend," she said sweetly, "this is a delightful surprise. I had not dared to hope that I should see you again so soon. Will you have wine, a *siroppo*, a cup of coffee? How did you come, by train or by car?"

"Nothing just now," he said, answering her last question but one. He sat down heavily for he was very tired, took out his cigarette case before he remembered that it was empty, and replaced it in his pocket with a sigh.

La Marucci smiled and offered hers, which was more than half full. Gualtieri took one. "You are always efficient, Amalia."

"Silvio keeps me well supplied."

"To be sure. In many ways a remarkable young man."

"I am glad you think so," she said lightly, but she looked at him under her lashes. How much had he heard about what was going on in Mont Alvino? It might be advisable to prepare him. "Poor boy. Just now he is trying so hard to—to act as a buffer between our people and the Germans. It is a thankless task."

"It must be."

She had moved away from the window. He got up and closed it and sat down again. His back was to the light and she could not see his face very clearly but she felt that he was watching her. She looked towards him as she unfurled her fan. She knew that her severely-cut black frock with its fine muslin collar and cuffs was very becoming. She was, of course, no longer young, but she was still a very handsome woman. She still had no doubt that this conversation would end as she meant that it should.

He said abruptly: "Silvio is convinced that the Germans will win the war?"

She was genuinely surprised. "Of course. They are so strong, and they have the advantage of inner lines of communication. The English and the Americans have to bring all their supplies by sea. It is a handicap they car never hope to overcome."

"They landed in Italy."

"And they are being pushed back again."

"That is what one is told," he agreed. "'What exactly do Silvio's friends—do the Germans expect to find in Mont Alvino? I heard that they were carrying out a house to house search."

"They are very angry about the blowing up of the tunnel. It is very natural. This was a very useful loop line, and a train full of German infantry was buried under the debris. They are saying that an English plane passed over here a week or two before, and crashed in the mountains, and there are rumours that one or two parachutists were dropped a few minutes previously. Silvio says the Germans think they carried out the sabotage and that they had been and perhaps still are hidden in the town. They are threatening all kinds of reprisals, but he hopes to keep them within bounds."

"That is very good of him."

Amalia was a clever woman, but she was insensitive, the finer shades of meaning often passed unnoticed by her. She answered warmly, suspecting no irony.

"It is the least he can do. He feels that the people here are his people by adoption. Thanks to your kindness this is his home. You don't know how deeply he respects you, how grateful he is. He does not show his feelings." The marchese said nothing, and for some minutes there was no sound in the room but the ticking of the gilt Empire clock on the mantelpiece and the gentle rhythmic rustling of Amalia's fan.

She was still so far from gauging his mood that she thought he was making up his mind to ask her to marry him. She thought, "When the war is over, I'll make him let the Villa and open up the *piano nobile* of the palace in Rome. With Silvio's help I could be one of the political hostesses. An Embassy—with Silvio to do the real work and the old fool as a figurehead. How old is he? Sixty? And I am not much over forty."

Gualtieri, looking at her, felt that he was looking at a stranger. Unconsciously and by degrees he had come to depend for so much on the woman he had believed her to be, the loyal affectionate devoted creature whom he had left in entire charge of his dead son's wife and child. Now he had lost what, actually, he had never had. She was plausible, but he knew he could never be deceived again. Still, for his own satisfaction, to make sure, he would have to induce her to betray herself if it was only by an unguarded movement.

Deliberately he looked about him at the walls panelled in faded green brocade and hung with even more faded landscapes in water-colour by his grandmother who had come to the Villa as a bride a hundred years ago. "Lucia—my wife, liked to sit in this room. That was before your time, before her last illness."

"Poor dear Donna Lucia," sighed Amalia.

"She died, the doctor said, of a duodenal ulcer. I have been wondering lately if he was mistaken."

He was watching her hands and he saw the knuckle: whiten as her fingers gripped the fan.

"How could that be?"

"I think she may have been poisoned by arsenic, not with one large fatal dose as in the case of, Chiara, but little by little. Yes. I think she may have been killed by inches."

"You are not serious. What possible motive—who would do such a thing? Everyone loved her."

"I thought so certainly. But Chiara was gentle and harmless too, and yet she died."

"Yes. But in her case there was an understandable motive. She knew too much about Alda Olivieri's love affair.

I couldn't believe at first that Alda was guilty but now I do. The wretched girl is a nymphomaniac. That is the evident explanation."

"She knew too much. I agree with you there. But I am not so sure that this dangerous knowledge concerning her young cousin."

The warning bell had rung at last for Amalia. Mechanically she closed her fan and laid it down. She said nothing but sat quite still, waiting. Only her eyes moved from the door to the window and back again.

"I see that you understand me," he said. "Your past, I could forget that if, from the moment my wife and I received you, there had been an end to the plotting and scheming. Lucia was good to you, generous and kind but she was in your way. You had to be mistress here."

"You are mad," she said. "I shall call for help."

"You will not be heard. You are afraid? How right you are," he said, smiling. "And you were so near your goal, too. Only the other day my sister, the Reverend Mother, asked me if I meant to marry you, and I said I was considering it."

"You think I would have consented? You flatter yourself," she said.

"Oh, only as a means to an end. Before long, no doubt, I should have had digestive trouble. Why are you listening? Do you hear anything?"

She moistened her lips. "No."

"You are expecting a visit from Silvio perhaps? Do you want to say a prayer?"

She shook her head. "You are quite quite wrong. I don't know how you got these ideas. You—you are not well. The shock of that poor child's death—"

He withdrew his right hand from his coat pocket. "This is Amedeo's pistol. It was sent to me with his other possessions after his death."

"Listen. I swear to you, I swear that I have done nothing. Whoever told you—it is all a lie. For God's sake. You must believe me."

"I do not believe you."

"You dare not touch me. You'll be arrested, charged with murder. What about your precious grandson then with Silvio as his only surviving relative? Silvio's not much use with children. He doesn't like them—"

She was talking at random, playing for time. Her strained eyes turned again to the window, still hoping to see the slim figure of her son. He would be quick to act, she knew. She opened her mouth wide and screamed at the top of her voice. "Silvio! *Aiuto! Aiuto!*"

The two old servants in the kitchen heard two shots just after the scream. Their eyes met. Caterina fumbled for her rosary in her apron pocket.

Amalia had toppled sideways from her chair. Gualtieri, who was still seated, got up slowly and stiffly and went over to her. He said to himself: "Two bullets in her brain. One would have been enough. It was too quick a death."

He dragged the body into a corner of the room, away from the window, and pushed it behind a settee. The exertion had made him sweat profusely and he was out of breath. There was very little blood.

A few minutes later Pietro, disobeying orders, came upstairs and found his master sitting in his usual high-backed chair in the library. He was very pale and complained of feeling cold.

Pietro made him drink a little brandy and fetched a black cloth cape and a rug to put over his knees.

"I felt a little faint. Stupid of me. I have just remembered I have had nothing to eat since breakfast."

"Lasci fare—" Pietro fetched bread and wine and stood by while he ate and drank.

"That is better." A faint colour had come back to the lean bearded cheeks. "I suppose actually I am suffering from shock. You have asked no questions, Pietro. Have you no curiosity? You heard, I suppose?"

"*Sua Eccelenza* will tell me what he wishes me to know."

"A very proper spirit. Tell me, Pietro, are you and Caterina satisfied that Signorina Alda poisoned the Marchesina's lemonade?"

"No, Eccelenza, since you ask, we have never believed it."

"Whom did you suspect?"

Pietro eyed his master warily. "We are only servants, poor and ignorant—"

"You were afraid of her? I see. You suspected Donna Amalia?"

Pietro hesitated a moment. Then he said: "She hated the marchesina, and the signorina Alda too. I have seen it in her face when their backs were turned and she watched them go, when they walked arm in arm and laughed together. You never saw her as she really was, padrone. But now— now you know?"

"You heard the shots. I killed her. I fought in the war, in 1915, but I have never killed a woman before."

"Si, signore." The old servant's tone was matter of fact, but he looked worried. "What do we do now?"

Gualtieri let the rug slip off his knees. He felt warmer now and as if he could sleep. "Do?" he said. "I don't know."

He closed his eyes. Pietro stared at him helplessly. The great book-lined room was very quiet, the only sound a bee buzzing on the window pane. Superficially it was a peaceful scene, but it was a peace as brittle as blown glass. It was shattered by the ringing of the front door bell.

CHAPTER XVII
DEATH AT THE FARM

EVER since day broke Richard Drew had been sitting astride a branch of a chestnut tree.

It was a good strategic position. He was some way up, well screened by leaves, and not at all likely to be noticed by anyone passing below, and he had a clear view of the white walls and red tiled roof of the Donatis' farm-house across the clearing.

It was there that his adventures had begun. He had lost count of time and hardly knew if it was three weeks or three months ago. His cuts and bruises had healed, but, on the other hand, he must have lost at least a stone in weight. He had lived for the last few days entirely on chestnuts picked up in the woods. He had even been reduced to chewing grass and leaves. Aristide, he knew, would have found some edible fungi, but they all looked poisonous to him and he left them alone.

His plan, so far as he had a plan, was to attract the attention of Marietta and to find out from her what was happening to Alda.

After that—his mind refused to dwell on remote contingencies. He might be caught. Twice while he was still hidden in the Etruscan tomb he had heard men passing overhead and beating the undergrowth, and twice the same thing had happened after he had left his sanctuary and taken to the trees. Luckily it never seemed to occur to them to look up. Occasionally he heard shots or a quick rattle of machine guns coming apparently from the direction of the town, but he had not connected these sounds with the search.

He was fairly comfortable on his branch. He could lean back when he liked and rest his back against the trunk. He was much bitten by flies and mosquitoes, but that might be a good thing for the irritation kept him awake in spite of the drowsy heat of the afternoon. Most of the time he was chewing a chestnut—there were still a few left in his pocket—and as they were very dry they required a great deal of mastication before the could be swallowed.

Sooner or later he would be taken. He tried not to think of the things Germans, and probably Fascists, did to prisoners when they wanted them to talk. Very hard to know how much one could stand until one had actually been through the experience. Pain. That gnawing pain in the pit of his stomach for instance. Indigestion, or just plain hunger. He ought to be getting used to it, he had had it long enough. He rubbed himself cautiously. Aristide. He missed Aristide. Poor little Tonietta. He would never see her in the cash desk of that Soho restaurant of their dreams.

He looked impatiently towards the farm. He had seen them all during the day. Old Donati had come out to milk the tethered goat. A little later his wife had hung some washing on the line, and Marietta had appeared once, with the baby in her arms, to stand for a few minutes where the path turned downhill before she went in again. He dared not call out or try to attract their attention by any movement. After nightfall it might be safe to climb down and knock at their door.

It was strange, perhaps, that Alda had come to mean so much to him, Alda, whom he had seen only twice for a few minutes. They had reached intimacy through their daily exchange of letters. He had Don Luigi to thank for that. The old priest had told him why he consented to act as a go between. As the girl's spiritual director he had learned a good deal of her life at the Villa. He knew that she was not happy there, and that it was unlikely that any plans had been made for her future, "If you are sure of yourself and your feelings, my son—"

. Richard had answered that he was sure. And now Don Luigi, who, in his humble way, had guided, advised and tried to protect her, was gone. And the thing which he seemed to have feared had happened.

Alda had been involved in some dark and complicated intrigue in the household in which she had lived as a dependent. Accused of murder.

Murder.

Richard edged himself forward a few inches and shuffled back again. Pins and needles. Cramp. He shook his head irritably, trying to dislodge the mosquitoes settling on his face and neck. His memory, seeking relief, sidestepped all recent events, his training, his billets, the friends he had made and lost, the girls he had danced and dined with, even that red-haired WAAF—her name was Edith—and discovered a holiday spent at Beer, in Devon, when he was about eight years old, a holiday when the sun always shone and there were shrimps for tea, and the object of his hero worship, a good-natured fisherman, allowed him to sit by him on the beach and help to mend nets that smelt deliciously of tar.

Bathing at low tide, exploring rock pools. By some alchemy of the mind he could almost get back into that small compact eight-year-old body splashing happily in a few inches of sea water.

He was recalled to the present and its dangers by the sounds of a party of men approaching through the woods, crashing heavily through the undergrowth and talking excitedly. Germans. There was no mistaking those harsh guttural voices. Presently they passed underneath and crossed the clearing, going towards the farm. Two officers walked in front, big men, heavily built, with the thick red necks and square heads of typical Prussians. Their companion was a slim, dandified young fellow in a smartly-cut black Fascist uniform, one hand resting on the revolver hanging in a polished black leather holster from his belt. His head was bare, and his thick fair hair shone like gold in the sunlight. He moved with a self-conscious grace which the unseen observer in the tree found faintly nauseating. This trio were followed by six German soldiers. One of them carried over his arm an airman's sheepskin-lined coat, stained with earth and blackened with smoke, and a helmet with goggles.

Richard's heart sank. The Donati had buried his stuff, but evidently not deep enough since these men had found it. How far away? He feared that it was not far. What next? And what could he do? Obviously he could do nothing.

The flight of stone steps leading to the living-rooms on the first floor was on the other side of the house. Richard had to guess at what was going on. The Germans barking questions, the cracked quavering voice of the charcoal burner replying, the plangent tones of his wife intervening, pleading, protesting. They knew nothing of his present whereabouts, they would deny having hidden him, but they would not be believed. They were hopelessly implicated by the discovery of the leather coat so near the little farm. The inquisition went on and on, while the shadows lengthened across the sunbaked stony ground of the clearing, and the tethered goat, anxious to be milked, bleated impatiently.

A harmless old couple, pottering about their holding, living on their scanty crops of olives and maize and the sale of charcoal, and their daughter with a child in her arms. Surely it was not necessary to bring such a parade of force to overawe them? They were being bullied, threatened—

A woman—Marietta or her mother—screamed. Several shots rang out.

Richard gripped the branch before him convulsively. Nothing. Nothing to be done. A moment of complete silence was followed by one of the raucous German voices shouting orders. Two of the soldiers came round from the back of the house, opened the door of the empty cowshed and peered in. Richard noticed that they carried their guns at the ready and that their bayonets were fixed.

The goat was still bleating pitifully. One of the men came over to her, stabbed her several times, and turned away laughing, leaving her dying in a pool of blood and milk.

Richard ground his teeth. He was infuriated by his own helplessness. The rest of the party reappeared, apparently in high spirits. They did not take the path that led down the hill to the Villa, as he had thought they might, but retraced their steps across the clearing, returning the way they had come. As they approached and passed beneath his tree he noticed that the young Fascist was no longer with them.

Was it possible, he wondered, that the boy had intervened to protect his compatriots, and that his allies had turned on him? That question was answered in the negative soon after the echoes of Teutonic mirth had died away in the distance. The elegant black-clad figure of the young Fascist came briskly round the house with an armful of faggots which he deposited in the cowshed. He made three journeys, each time laden. After the last trip he spent several minutes in the shed. When he came out he left the door partly open and standing back lit a cigarette and waited for results. After perhaps a minute a thin wisp of smoke drifted out and rose in the still air.

He watched it for a moment, and then, treading lightly like a ballet dancer, moved away and vanished round the corner of the house.

"God!" said Richard, "he's going to burn the place down. Why?"

At that instant he heard quite distinctly the crying of a child.

Richard dropped to a lower branch and from there to the ground. He was stiff and clumsy after so many hours spent in a cramped position. His mouth was dry and he felt rather dizzy, but he could not waste time limbering up. If the Fascist came back while he was crossing the patch of open ground, he would be a perfect target, but if he reached the house he would stand a fair chance.

Normally he would be more than a match for the young Italian, but he was in poor condition, half-starved and worn out. He had gained a factitious strength, however, from his growing fury. Luck was with him, for he crossed the clearing unchallenged and crept round the house, keeping close to the wall. As he passed the cowshed he picked up a billet of wood which had been used to prop the door open. He could see a flicker of flame in the darkness within. There was straw there with the faggots and the fire had caught hold so that already clouds of smoke were billowing out. He turned the corner and saw all that there was to see.

The young Fascist had his back to him, he was sitting at the foot of the flight of steps leading to the upper floor, smoking his cigarette. A few feet away the bodies of Donati and his wife and daughter lay on the dusty earth. They had been riddled with bullets and already their faces were black with flies. At the top of the steps the door of the living-room and kitchen stood open. A bonfire of straw and faggots had been built across the threshold and smoke was rising from it. The crackling of the burning wood was loud enough to cover the sound of Richard's footsteps as he approached.

He brought the log he carried down with all his might on that golden head, but the other had a reptilian swiftness of movement, he swerved just in time and the blow glanced off his shoulder, dislocating his left arm and breaking the collar bone. He sprang up howling with mingled pain and rage. A confused struggle followed for the possession of the pistol which the Fascist had managed to draw. He fought like a wild cat, biting and scratching when his weapon had been twisted out of his hand. The end came when he slipped at the moment when Richard's fist caught him on the point of the chin. He fell back, striking the back of his head against the house wall. Richard stood over him, wild-eyed, sweating, his breath coming in great gasps. "Come on," he mumbled, "come on, you murdering little blighter—" but his opponent lay still, his head twisted at an unnatural angle, his bright hair streaked with dust and blood. His neck was broken.

The child was still crying, a thin persistent wailing. Richard stumbled up the steps and kicked aside the pile of brushwood that had been laid across the threshold just as it was beginning to blaze up. Already the room within was full of smoke, and the charcoal stove on which a pot of onion stew was coming to the boil, glowed dimly through the bluish haze. Richard dropped to his hands and knees and crawled across to the door of the inner room.

The place was very bare and poverty-stricken, but spotlessly clean. A photograph of Marietta's soldier husband was pinned to the wall over her bed by the stoup of holy water and the little shelf on which stood a gaily painted plaster statuette of the Madonna dei Sette Dolori. The wooden cradle stood by the bedside. Richard was beginning to cough and his eyes were smarting. He snatched up the baby, wrapped it awkwardly in a sheet snatched from the bed, and blundered out again.

He had a vague idea that the Germans might return, but there was no sign of them. He laid the child down on the ground and then, after a glance at the three bodies lying together by the foot of the steps, he plunged back through the thickening clouds of smoke and came back with another sheet to cover them.

There was a well. When he was lying in the cowshed he had often heard the creaking of the windlass. The water, he remembered, was always ice-cold. He drew up a bucketful, drank some, and bathed his face and hands. "God!" he said aloud, "I needed that."

His actions so far had been almost entirely instinctive, but now he began to think.

The baby was, of course, the child of Alda's cousin, and doubly orphaned now. There must be someone down at the

Villa who would take charge of it, and he would have to take it there since it was obviously impossible to leave it in that place of death. He felt no compunction about searching the body of the young Fascist and he took possession of his pistol in its holster and a wicked-looking knife in a leather sheath as well as a smart black morocco wallet stamped with the initials S.M. in gold and stuffed with papers, and a gold cigarette case engraved with the same initials.

Mercifully the baby had stopped crying and was lying where he had placed it, staring placidly up at the sky. He picked it up again, tucking it under his arm as he would have carried a dog, and took the downhill path to the Villa. But first he cast a final glance round the clearing which in the last hour had been the scene of a tragedy as sombre and complete as any devised by an Elizabethan dramatist. The fire, he thought, was dying down, but wisps of smoke still drifted from the doors and windows. The silence was oppressive. The only living things that remained were a few scraggy fowls scratching forlornly in the dust as they waited in vain for the handful of grain Marietta had always thrown to them before she shut them up for the night.

In the west the sun was setting in a blaze of glory.

CHAPTER XVIII
THE LOAN OF A PIANO

PIETRO had closed the library door as he went out. The marchese listened but could not hear the voices of the visitor or visitors in the hall. Who were they? He had no idea. He leaned back in his chair and shut his eyes. Presently, when he had rested, he would be able to think more clearly.

155 | DEATH AT THE VILLA

He opened his eyes again to find Pietro standing beside him. The old man moved noiselessly in his felt house slippers.

"Padrone, padrone, it is the bambino. A stranger has brought him—"

Gualtieri looked towards the door and saw a lean, haggard, dishevelled object clad in a filthy shirt and torn linen trousers and holding what appeared to be a small bundle of laundry.

Richard felt as if he had stepped into an illustration for *Don Quixote* among his books. He grinned disarmingly at the picturesque and rather formidable figure in the high-backed carved chair as he moved forward.

"Beg pardon, sir, if this is an intrusion. Do you speak English by any chance?"

Gualtieri stared. "Yes. You are English?"

"I am. Thank God you can understand me. It will be easier to explain."

The bundle in his arms stirred and whimpered. Richard glanced down at it. "Hold on, pal. You are the marchese Gualtieri?"

"Yes."

"Then this is your grandson. If there is any woman about who can cope with him. I'd be glad to hand him over."

"Pietro, fetch Caterina."

The old manservant hurried away.

Gualtieri was wide awake now. His eyes were keen and wary as they searched the Englishman's face. "You are the man—or one of the men they have been looking for? You blew up the bridge?"

"Do I have to answer that?"

"Perhaps not. It is more important to me to know what you are doing with that child. How do you know he is my grandson?"

"I was hiding up in the woods. I've been all day up a tree near the Donatis' farm."

"You knew Donati?"

"They sheltered me for some days after the plane crashed. They were kind to me."

"I see. Go on."

They were interrupted by Caterina coming in like a whirlwind.

"What is all this? Pietro says—*anima benedetta!*" She snatched the baby from Richard's arms and carried it away, completely ignoring her master.

Gualtieri followed her with his eyes. "You must excuse her," he said, with the shadow of a smile. "She has spent all her life in our service. She is very devoted. But—what happened up there at the podere?"

"The Germans came and with them one of your people. I imagine he brought them. Unfortunately they had found a part of my kit. Marietta told me they had buried it, but they can't have dug deep enough. As to what happened, I could not see, but I heard talking and then several shots. The Germans left but the Fascist remained behind. I saw him stacking up brushwood and realised he was trying to burn the house down." He broke off. "May I sit down?"

"Of course. Of course. I am forgetting my manners. Forgive me."

Richard resumed. "The child was still in the house. I heard it crying. I climbed down from my tree and went over to investigate. I'm afraid this is bad news, sir—"

"I understand."

"The bodies of Donati and his wife and daughter were lying on the ground. They had been shot through the head. The—the fellow they left behind sat on the steps smoking a cigarette. I suppose he was waiting to make sure the fire took hold. We had a bit of a scrap, an all-in affair, the little devil bit me twice. He was as slippery as an eel and as savage as a wild cat, but I knocked him out eventually and he broke his neck."

"What was he like?"

"Remarkably good-looking in an effeminate sort of way. Small waist like a girl's and sleek golden hair. Quite a young chap."

"Silvio Marucci."

"I shouldn't be surprised," agreed Richard. "S.M. were the initials on his wallet and his very posh cigarette case. I suppose he would know your grandson was there with his foster-mother?"

"Naturally."

"If I hadn't been there and seen him the Jerries would have got the blame for the whole show. He's related to you, isn't he, sir? He might have expectations?"

"He might," said the marchese grimly. "Evidently I owe you the life of my grandson, a debt I can never hope to repay in full. But I will do what I can. You will honour me by staying here while we try to arrange for your escape to the Allied lines. I am alone here with the two servants you have seen, and you can trust them. They will not betray you."

"That's darned good of you, sir. It's a bit risky, you know. I'd be only too glad, of course. I'm pretty well all in. But— what about that chap's mother? I understood that she lived here. I—I've been in a devil of a stew all this time expecting her to walk in and ask who I am and what I've been doing—"

"Do not let that trouble you. Amalia Marucci is—is no longer here."

He rang the bell and Pietro answered it so promptly that it seemed not unlikely that he had been hovering in the hall, waiting for the summons.

The marchese gave him brief but sufficient instructions.

The signore was to be taken up to the bathroom and provided with plenty of warm water, a razor to shave with, and a complete change of clothing. He would be dining at the Villa and staying the night. Caterina was to do her best to provide an appetising meal.

Pietro looked anxiously at his master. "*Si, signore.* But as to clothes. Am I to take those that belonged to Don Amedeo?"

"Certainly. The marchesino would be only too glad to oblige this gentleman. He is an Englishman, Pietro, and he is in hiding. Tell Caterina. His presence here is a secret. *Capita?*"

"*Capita, Eccelenza.*"

Pietro, slightly dazed but obedient, conducted the tattered figure upstairs.

Chiara had never summoned up courage to go through the wardrobe and dressing-chest in her husband's dressing-room and sort out his clothes to be sent to various charitable organisations, and she had been unusually firm in refusing to allow Amalia Marucci to do it for her. "I won't have that woman prying about among Amedeo's things," she had told Alda. The old manservant pottered about, mumbling to himself. "Underwear and the grey lounge suit and the grey suede shoes—"

There was only a very small jug of hot water, but he had produced a carefully hoarded cake of scented soap.

Richard got rid of a good deal of grime in a cold tub and scraped nearly a week's beard off his jaws, a painful process but one that helped to restore his shaken morale. Pietro, remaining in attendance, cleansed the two ragged wounds on his arm with antiseptic and covered them with a bandage before helping him on with the shirt and coat.

"They might have been made for the signore—"

He looked up imploringly—"What has happened?"

Richard realised that though the old man had probably been listening at the door, he had been baffled by the fact that his conversation with the marchese had been carried on in English.

Richard told him the bare facts. His Italian was still imperfect but it sufficed. Pietro said nothing, but before he turned away Richard saw that the tears were running down his wrinkled cheeks.

Richard was left alone for a few minutes. He looked at his reflection in the mirror and wondered if any of his friends would recognise him. In three or four weeks he had aged ten years. The lined face with its hollow cheeks and sunken blue eyes was that of a man of thirty-five, a man, moreover, who was just recovering from a severe illness, with a waxen pallor under the sun tan.

He felt better, but still rather shaky and he was glad to sit down. He looked about him, taking stock of his surroundings.

Evidently this had been the dressing-room of the marchese's airman son. A drawer which Pietro had left half-open held a large assortment of ties. A photograph of a beautiful girl in a silver frame stood on the dressing-table. That would be Alda's cousin, the mother of the poor little scrap of humanity who, thanks to his chance arrival on the scene, might live to be old.

Pietro had carried away his rags. He returned with a small glass of cognac on a tray. "*Sua Eccelenza* advises you to drink this and then rest quietly here. I will fetch you when dinner is ready. There are Germans about searching the neighbourhood, but they are not likely to come here."

"Is there any place I can hide if they do?"

Pietro looked doubtful. "Inside the wardrobe perhaps. But they will not come. They—" he broke off to listen.

Richard drank his brandy in two gulps. "Don't be too sure. That's the front door bell. Pull yourself together, man, or your face will give the show away."

Pietro nodded. "Lock yourself in. I shall say I've lost the key."

He shambled away. Richard followed him to the door and turned the key in the lock. There was nothing more he could do and he was dead tired. He sat down again and within five minutes he was fast asleep.

Major Fritz Weiss jerked at the bell impatiently. He refused to allow himself to be overawed by the immense golden brown façade of the Villa Gualtieri. These Italians with their megalomaniac operatic backgrounds must be kept in their places.

He was a youngish, fattish man with thin, sandy hair cut too close to a typically Nordic pink scalp, piggy eyes under jutting brows and a wide, thin-lipped mouth. The two-seater in which he had come was drawn up at the foot of the steps leading to the main entrance. Behind it was an army lorry with its S.S. driver sitting stiffly at the wheel.

The door was opened rather slowly and reluctantly. Weiss, who was well used to this kind of reception, glanced without interest at the frail bent figure of the old manserv-ant in his faded livery.

"Tell Signor Marucci that Captain Weiss is here and that he has brought a lorry."

"Signor Marucci is not here, signore."

"Nicht?" Weiss was surprised and annoyed. "He should have arrived before this. He was to explain to his mother about the piano."

"He is not here."

"What the devil can he be doing?" Weiss spoke Italian fluently but with a harsh German accent. "Perhaps I had better see the lady."

He had visited the Villa once with Haussmann and Silvio Marucci. It was merely a social call. Donna Amalia had been very gracious. A handsome woman, though no longer young, and they had drunk the health of the Fuehrer in a really excellent wine. Self-consciously he smoothed down the wrinkles that were apt to spoil the set of his coat over his stomach and prepared to cross the threshold. But the old butler did not make way for him.

"I am sorry. Donna Amalia went to Rome this morning. She took a suitcase and said she might not be back for some days."

"And she has left you in charge?"

"Si, signore."

"Bene. Now listen. We are giving a party to-night at the hotel. The piano there is abominable. Marucci says you have a good one here, a small one, easy to move." He looked round at the lorry driver. "You there. Hans. Come up here and give the old fellow a hand with the instrument. Where is it?"

Pietro stared at him blankly. He was afraid, but he knew he must not let his fear be seen. Fortunately Weiss was insensitive and did not realise that there was anything amiss.

"Where is it?" he said again a little louder, supposing that the old servant was deaf.

Pietro moistened his lips. There seemed to be no way out. There was only one piano at the Villa. It had been one of the marchese's wedding presents to his daughter-in-law.

The little green morning-room. It was in there that he had heard them quarrelling—how long ago? an hour? He had lost count of time.

"One moment, signore. It is too dark to see indoors. If the signore will wait, I will fetch a lamp."

"Haven't you electric light in this barrack of a place?"

"No, signore."

The German's comment was a snort of amused contempt. The lorry driver came heavily up the steps to join him and they both watched Pietro cross the hall and light a brass lucerna standing on a table at the foot of the grand staircase whose wrought-iron balustrade curved up into the darkness.

Pietro was thinking. They did not know that the marchese had arrived that day at the Villa. If he remained in the library he might be kept out of any trouble that impended. If only he had had time to—to put things to rights. But there was nothing he could do now, and if he made excuses it would only arouse their suspicions. His gnarled work-worn hands shook as he struck a match and touched the three wicks of the lamp. His voice trembled as he said: "This way, signori—"

The two Germans were close at his heels as he entered the room. It was quite dark, for Gualtieri had closed the windows and drawn the long green brocade curtains before he left. The light from the lucerna did not extend very far. The three flames were reflected dimly and confusingly in the two oval mirrors in their Venetian frames, and in the glass of the faded water-colours hanging on the silk-panelled walls. The little gilt-legged chairs were arranged in a prim half-circle facing the sofa. Only Pietro, knowing the room so well, noticed that the sofa stood a little farther than was usual from the wall.

Weiss had gone directly to the piano, opened it, and struck a few chords. "Good," he said approvingly. "Good." He pulled out the music stool, sat down and played the little *minuet* by Beethoven. While he was playing his fat red face expressed a dreamy ecstasy. The lorry driver waited stolidly by the door, and Pietro stood unobtrusively shading the lamp so that the sofa remained in shadow. His chief fear was that Gualtieri would leave the library to find out what was going on.

Weiss got up. "It will do," he said brusquely. "Hans, you take one end. You, what's your name, give me the lamp."

It was a tedious business, for Pietro often had to set his end down and rest for a minute. The two younger men, seeing that he was far too weak to lift such a weight, grinned at each other, amused by his efforts. At last the piano was safely in the lorry. Pietro stood back, his thin body heaving like that of an overdriven horse. The driver climbed into his seat and Weiss went over to his car.

"If Marucci turns up later tell him he is expected at the Albergo Centrale. We mean to enjoy ourselves. Music, and we've collected some girls."

He pressed the self-starter and drove off. Hans, preparing to follow, saw a chance to assert his authority now that his superior officer had gone. "Take that lamp indoors," he snapped, "or I'll report you for signalling to the enemy."

Pietro answered dully, *"Si, signore,"* and shuffled back into the house, shutting the door after him.

Gualtieri came out of the library. "Pietro," he began, "what the devil—"

Pietro turned towards him and took two faltering steps before his knees gave way under him and he dropped to the floor.

Gualtieri, alarmed, shouted for Caterina. She came at once and between them they carried him into the dining-room where some time previously the table had been laid for Donna Amalia's solitary supper. His eyes opened after they had moistened his lips with cognac.

"Pardon, Eccelenza," he mumbled.

"It is I who should ask yours," said Gualtieri angrily, "for leaving you to face them alone. But I was afraid of making bad worse."

"You were right, Eccelenza. I prayed to San Pietro, to all the saints that you would not come out to them."

"What did they want?" asked Gualtieri curiously. "What was all that noise of moving furniture? I wondered—"

Pietro explained. "They took the piano, Donna Chiara's piano, for a party."

Their eyes met. "You knew what was behind the sofa?"

"I guessed, Eccelenza. Presently I will get a spade. There will be a moon later—"

Caterina interrupted. She seldom listened to her husband.

"I must go back to my kitchen or the risotto will burn. Lay another cover, Pietro. Dinner will be ready in ten minutes."

The marchese looked at her with some amusement, wondering how much she knew or understood of their position, which had been desperate a few minutes ago, and was still precarious.

"What have you done with my grandson, Caterina? He was very quiet during the recent visit of our allies."

"And a good thing too, if *sua Eccelenza* means those dirty German pigs. He's had a sup of goat's milk, bless him, and I found a basket that'll do for a cradle, and he's asleep in the pantry, which is the coolest place."

She bustled, away, and the two men watched her go.

"Does she know about la Marucci?"

"Yes. I told her. She said it was a good riddance. Whatever happens meals have to be cooked, and eaten, and cleared away. That's what Caterina says, and she's right. The German expected to find Signorino Silvio here," said Pietro uneasily, "if he comes—there is this Englishman—"

"He will not come."

Pietro looked enquiringly at his master. The marchese nodded. "I see," said Pietro more cheerfully. He went about his work, humming gently to himself as he moved round the table, setting another knife, fork and spoon, laying a lace mat on the polished wood, rearranging the roses in the crystal bowl and stepping back to judge the effect before he lit the candles in the great silver candelabra, unconsciously seeking relief from an unbearable tension by doing the ordinary everyday things that were part of a life-long routine.

Gualtieri watched him. He thought, "If they had found the body they would have taken him." Aloud he said: "You thought we would bury her in the garden?"

"Naturally. That must be done to-night."

"No, Pietro. I will not have you and Caterina involved in this affair which does not concern you. To-morrow morning I shall give myself up."

"The padrone is tired and hungry," said Pietro calmly. He moved a fork half an inch to the left. "After dinner he will think differently."

The marchese smiled in spite of himself. It was so exactly the tone in which Pietro used to promise to put his world to rights for a ten-year-old boy, to mend his scooter or get a kite down from the top of a tree.

"I don't think so," he said, "but I certainly am ready for dinner. You had better fetch down our visitor."

He had so far recovered from his first shock that he was able to observe his own reactions to violent death with detached interest. He felt much less than he would have expected. Perhaps, he thought, he was to some extent stunned by succeeding blows.

He was sitting in his place at the head of the table when Richard Drew came in. His heart seemed to miss a beat. He remembered that grey suit very well. In the dim candlelight he could almost fancy he saw Amedeo. But the Englishman was not really like him.

Gualtieri remembered his duties as a host.

"Sit here, on my right. I hope you are rested—"

Pietro served the soup.

CHAPTER XIX
CONVERSATION AT A SUPPER TABLE

THE soup was followed by a dish of artichokes baked in batter and by a very small roast chicken with a contorno of beans and tiny new potatoes. Gualtieri talked a little of a visit he had paid to England in nineteen hundred and ten. Richard was politely attentive and tried not to wolf his food. There was no sweet, but Pietro brought in a dish of nespoli and oranges and refilled their glasses with wine before he left the room.

"I am sorry there is no coffee," said Gualtieri. "I do not care for the substitute. This wine—does it seem sour to you? It is from my own vineyard on the hillside."

"I'm not a judge of wines," said Richard. "I drink beer at home. The food was marvellous. I've been living on raw chestnuts lately."

The marchese eyed him reflectively. Not a bad-looking young fellow, and evidently a gentleman.

"There is a good deal about this affair that I do not yet understand. You say you were hidden by Donati after the crash of your plane. Were there any other survivors?"

"One. He is dead now."

"You saved my grandson's life. Was it your impression that the young fellow you fought with and killed meant to burn down the podere with the child in it?"

"I'm sure of it," said Richard. "It was the most cold-blooded thing I ever saw. I suppose his German pals would have been blamed for it, and they might not have known there was a child in the place. I did not hear him crying while they were there."

"Did you wonder why he was taking some trouble to destroy a baby a few months old?"

"I thought I could make a guess. I had heard a good deal about the set-up here from Alda."

The marchese stared at him. "Alda. What do you know of her?"

Richard told him. It was rather a long story, but Gualtieri listened to him with the closest attention.

"So that was it," he said at last. "Amalia said she was hiding something. She was right in that. But I don't see how this is going to help. Was it because of her that you have not tried to get away?"

"Yes. I heard she had been arrested for the murder of her cousin. I knew there must be some mistake. I had to find out what was happening. To-day I was watching the podere hoping to get hold of Marietta and learn something from her."

"My daughter-in-law was poisoned. There was arsenic in the lemonade which Alda had prepared and taken up to her room. The suggested motive was that Chiara had threatened to tell her duenna and myself of Alda's illicit love affair. Amalia contrived to hint at something of the sort while protesting that the girl was innocent."

"I can't imagine how anyone who knew Alda could believe it for a moment," said Richard hotly.

"I trusted Signora Marucci. I relied on her judgment. I only learned her true character yesterday. That is why I came here to-day."

"Where is she?" Richard had wanted to ask this question before.

Gualtieri sat looking down at the dregs of wine in his glass. "On my way here I called at the Prefettura. I saw the prefetto who is an old friend of mine. I told him that as regards Amalia Marucci I had been entirely deceived, that there were witnesses in Venice, including the Venetian police, who could prove that she and her husband had run a gambling den, and that after his death she had black-mailed some of their former patrons, while her son Silvio had an even worse reputation; and that my daughter-in-law had been in correspondence with someone who knew these facts and probably intended to inform me. I asked that Alda should be released from custody and la Marucci arrested. He told me it was impossible. He dared not do it. His reason was that Silvio Marucci had too much influence with the Party and too many powerful friends among the Germans."

"I get it," said Richard. "You can hardly blame him."

"No," said Gualtieri heavily. "I did not blame him. I know that in Italy there is no law, there is no justice. If men complain of abuses or extortion they disappear. My friend the prefetto is as honest as he can afford to be. He said so himself."

Richard said nothing. The silence of the great house was oppressive. The table at which they sat, with its lace mats and gleaming silver, and the wax candles burning in the tall silver candelabra was like an oasis in a desert of black and white tiles. Dim shapes beckoned and fled on the frescoed walls. It was like a setting for the last act of *Don Giovanni*. The marchese, a formidable figure in his black clothes, rigidly upright in his carved chair, had the air of a Spanish grandee, of the Commander.

"You asked me where she is," Gualtieri finished his wine and set down the glass with a steady hand. "She is in the next room. She pretended to make me welcome. I questioned her and she tried to fence with me, but her guilt was written in her face. False, false as hell. I had brought my son's service revolver with me. One bullet as she tried to escape, a second as she lay at my feet to make sure."

"Good God!" muttered Richard.

"It was too quick, too easy," said Gualtieri harshly. "Chiara was not so fortunate. I intend to give myself up to-morrow morning. But meanwhile we must decide what can be done for you. I think we must consult Pietro. He may have some ideas. He is very intelligent."

"Anything you say, sir. But what about Alda? What can be done about her? That's the main thing. They may let her go, but what is to become of her if you are arrested? This was her only home, wasn't it?"

The marchese eyed him thoughtfully. "You are serious about this young girl, Captain—"

"Sergeant—"

"Sergeant Drew. You have seen her twice for a few minutes, you have carried on a clandestine correspondence. No doubt you are grateful to her for her assistance, for risking her life. They wouldn't hesitate to shoot her, you know, for aiding an enemy. Perhaps she didn't realise the danger. She is very young and of a romantic disposition, it seems. To tell you the truth, I scarcely know her though she has lived in my house as my daughter-in-law's friend and companion."

"I'm grateful, of course," said Richard, "but it isn't that. I—she's different to any girl I've played about with. If I get out of this jam, if I live, I want her to marry me." He wanted to say: "I love her," but he could not get it out. Gualtieri nodded. He had heard of the English habit of understatement and he had not expected raptures.

"Bene," he said dryly. "We will leave it at that, and come back to the immediate present and its very pressing problems."

He rang the bell, and when the old manservant came in he told him to sit down. "We need your advice, *amico mio.*" He turned to Richard. "You are willing that I should tell him all you have told me?"

"I am in your hands, sir."

Gualtieri talked for about five minutes. Richard found it difficult to follow his rapid Italian, but now and again he picked up a familiar name. Marietta, Don Luigi, Donna Amalia. He had given the marchese a condensed version of his adventures, avoiding as far as possible any reference to Aristide Pellico and his relatives. The fewer people he implicated the better. Nothing could hurt Don Luigi now, or Marietta and her parents. He reflected gloomily that of the eight people with whom he had been in contact since he crawled out of the wrecked plane five were dead and one in prison. In prison—but not, thank God, for helping him. He could only hope that nothing had happened to Tonietta and her father.

"Drew?"

"Yes, sir?"

"I think you said you went through Silvio Marucci's pockets and brought away his wallet?"

"His wallet, his cigarette case and his wrist-watch."

"Let me see the wallet."

The marchese flicked contemptuously at the little gilt coronet stamped on the black morocco leather over the monogram. "He had no right to that. These papers may be of interest." He looked through them carefully. "I think these prove that he belonged to the OVRA, the secret police," he said presently. "A permit to requisition motor fuel, a pass for himself and his car signed by the Duce himself and countersigned by the Germans. No wonder the prefetto was afraid of him. We ought to be able to make some use of these. I wonder where his car is. In the garage of the Albergo Centrale, I suppose."

Pietro leaned forward eagerly. "No, Eccelenza. He left it here at the Villa. I heard him tell his mother he would not need it. She was urging him not to make himself too conspicuous in the town while the hunt for hostages was going on as it would be remembered against him later on.

They would not notice him in a car with the Germans as they would if he drove himself."

The marchese pulled at his beard thoughtfully. "Can you drive a car, Drew?"

"I've never driven one of an Italian make, but I expect I could soon get the hang of it. You mean I might take a chance with his papers?"

"There might be a chance. It depends on when his body is found. It will be found, I presume? You did not put it inside the house?"

"I'm afraid not, I left it lying where he fell at foot of the steps."

"His German friends will look for him."

"Not to-night, I think, Eccelenza," said Pietro. "The one who came here just now to fetch the piano talked of a party and girls. They will be too busy amusing themselves to-night."

Gualtieri glanced at the Englishman's weary face. "You are tired out. A long drive through the night along roads you do not know, and, at any moment, an incident in which you would have to play your part. No. We must think of something else," he said with a sigh.

Richard, who had been smothering a yawn, jerked himself upright. "I'm afraid I'm pretty well all out," he admitted ruefully. "But one can generally squeeze out another ounce if one's put to it. I'd be all right after a few hours' sleep."

Gualtieri translated for Pietro's benefit. The old mar shook his head. "There's not time for that. Didn't he say the podere was burning? If the smoke is seen people may be on their way there now. If they are *brava gente*—decent folk—they will keep their mouths shut and pretend they haven't been near the place when they see what has happened; but

if they are Fascists they will report at once to the authorities in the town."

"There's another point," said Richard. "I can make myself
understood in Italian, and I get a general idea of what is
being said, but I couldn't possibly pass for a native."

A slow smile dawned on Gualtieri's grave face and trans-
formed it. "Leave it to me," he said. "I have an idea, several
ideas, in fact." He looked at his watch. "We must not start
too soon. We must allow the party at the Centrale to become
sufficiently immersed in wine, women and song. You can
lie down on the bed in my son's dressing-room. Pietro will
rouse you when it is the moment to make ready. Meanwhile
I will work out the details of my plan."

"Look here, sir," said Richard earnestly, "I don't want you
to take any risks on my account. You've got to be here and
not under suspicion. Who else is there to look after Alda?"

Gualtieri laid a friendly hand on his shoulder. "Don't
worry. It will amuse me to prove myself a man of action. All
these years I have shut myself up with my books. Now—we
shall see. And you will do as you are told. *Sono io il padrone.*"

Chapter XX
POLICE AT THE VILLA

"But at this hour," said the nun indignantly. "Surely they
could wait until the morning? She is still in the infirmary.
Her nerves are in a bad state."

"I have to carry out my orders, Suora Marta. She is to
be removed to another prison and at once. No use asking
me why."

"These men," scolded the nun, "they have no pity and no decency. I will ring up the doctor. He will not allow it."

The man grinned. "You are too soft-hearted, *Suora mia*. All this fuss over a murderess."

"That child is no murderess. Wait—" she picked up the telephone on the office desk, and dialled a number.

The warder shrugged his shoulders impatiently, but he waited. The doctor, apparently, was at home. The nun explained the circumstances.

"They want to remove one of the women prisoners, a patient in the infirmary, to-night. Alda Olivieri. Will you forbid it? She is asleep, naturally, at this time of night. The reason? They say they have received information that she is to be helped to escape. What did you say? Ridiculous. Yes, of course." She covered the mouthpiece and turned to the warder who lounged against the wall picking his teeth. "Who are these people? He wants to know."

"How should I know. They are high up." He came nearer and prudently lowered his voice to a hoarse whisper. "Friends of that little scab, Silvio Marucci. He's in the car with them. He's been hurt. His head is bandaged."

Suora Marta passed this information on to the doctor in more suitable terms, listened, frowning, to his reply, and hung up the receiver.

"He says he can do nothing. I shall try the prefetto. I know he takes a special interest in the case."

"And what am I to say to them for keeping them waiting?" growled the warder.

Suora Marta ignored him. She sat at her desk, a dignified figure in her black habit, her starched white linen coif framing her kind old face, frowning partly through anxiety and partly in the effort to hear. The prefetto's wife had come to the telephone, and, being voluble by nature, was not easy to get rid of, but in time she was persuaded to fetch her husband. The conversation that ensued was almost word for word what, had gone before. The warder listened grinning. "Nothing doing?" he said as she hung up.

"Nothing." Her lips moved silently for a moment before she stood up. "Very well. I will get her ready for her journey. Did they say where they are taking her?"

"No. Be as quick as you can, *Suora, mia benedetta*. I will wait in the corridor."

He followed her up the stone stairs, closed at the top and the bottom with iron gates which she opened with keys hanging from her belt with her rosary, and along a passage smelling of disinfectants to the door of the infirmary.

A nightlight burned before a picture of the Virgin. On the opposite wall there was a large poster of the Duce in smiling conversation with a group of peasant women with children clinging to their skirts. Three of the beds were occupied. The nun went to one of them and gently touched the brown head on the pillow.

"Wake up, my dear."

Reluctantly Alda opened her eyes. "Morning, already?"

"No, my child. You are to get up. Here are your clothes. Come, I will help you."

Alda had been given a mild sedative after several disturbed nights and its effects would not wear off yet. Half dazed she allowed herself to be huddled into her clothes, and sat on the side of the bed while the nun packed the little week-end case which was all she had brought with her to the prison.

"Am I being released?"

Her heart sank at, the prospect. Was she to go back to the Villa, to Donna Amalia? She had no other home, She sighed with relief when the nun said gently: "Not just yet, my child. You are being moved. I can only advise you to be docile and obedient as you have been here."

"You have been kind. I would rather stay here."

The nun was fastening the straps of the little case. "There. Now we will kneel and say a little prayer together before you go." They were still on their knees when the warder, losing patience, rapped on the door.

Suora Marta took her patient into the corridor, gently supporting her with an arm about her waist, and might have gone farther, but one of the other women had woke up and was moaning and she had to turn back to attend to her.

The warder took her case from her and hurried her down the stairs, holding her arm to prevent her from falling. He was not grinning now. He had not realised how young she was. Perhaps, after all, the nun was right. Why should she be moved like this, secretly and by night, when she was not a political prisoner? Marucci had his authority from the highest quarters, he was well thought of in Rome apparently, but everyone in Mont Alvino knew the boy was a nasty piece of work. But there was nothing he could do about it.

It was dark in the street and the headlights of the car were dimmed. Marucci, his head heavily bandaged, sat stiffly in the driver's seat. The other man seated beside him said curtly: "Put her in the back."

He scarcely had time to close the door before the car started and he had to spring back to avoid being caught by the mudguard. He cursed Marucci and the OVRA, but not so that he could be overheard.

The prefetto, meanwhile, was even more worried than his subordinate. He had hung up the receiver after his conversation with Suora Marta and sat back frowning and biting his nails. He could hear his wife in the next room moving about heavily as she prepared for bed. Presently she would be grumbling and complaining, preventing him from getting any sleep. It was always difficult to make her understand how careful he had to be. He was glad now that they had sent the three girls to their aunt in Pistoia. The country had come to a pretty pass when officials of his standing could be flouted and the processes of the law set aside by a young good-for-nothing like Silvio Marucci. He thought over what had passed between him and the marchese that afternoon. If Gualtieri had gone on from the Prefecture to the Villa he must have seen Amalia Marucci and, quite possibly, her son. Had he accused them both of murdering Chiara? If so, the removal of Alda to another, an unknown place of detention was a very likely counter move.

Would he be such a fool? The prefetto thought it probable. He had always liked and admired the marchese, but he was not blind to his faults. He was used to having his own way. He had never taken any part in politics and he was not rich enough to be worth fleecing, so the Fascist Party had not interfered with him hitherto. During the last two years he might have owed his immunity to young Marucci, a fact that would deeply wound his pride if he ever became aware of it. The prefetto had seen that he still had very little conception of the real position. To him Amalia Marucci and her son were merely poor relations whom he had succoured and who had shamefully abused his kindness while deceiving him as to their character. He was slow to understand that prudence would be necessary when dealing with them.

"He rushed off," thought the prefetto, sighing, "like a bull charging the matador's cloak."

He had been firm with the infirmary sister. The only safe course now was to remain as aloof as possible from this involved and tragic affair. He was, in fact, absolved, for once the dreaded OVRA took charge there was nothing more to be said or done. And yet—he eyed the telephone uncertainly. He was a kind-hearted man, and he had daughters of his own. He could not forget Alda's strained and anxious eyes, the quivering of those soft young lips as they tried to answer the questions he had to ask.

"No. No. I wouldn't have hurt Chiara. Not for the world. I loved her. Oh, poor Chiara."

He wanted very much to know what had happened at the Villa. If only the marchese had not been so prejudiced against all such modern inventions as electric light and the telephone.

His wife called to him from the inner room. "Ercole. Aren't you ever coming to bed?"

"*Subito. Subito.*"

He switched off the lamp on his desk and opened the shutters. Across the piazza the Duomo loomed black against a sky bright with stars. No lights were to be seen anywhere. There was an occasional rumbling, only just audible, which might have been distant thunder of guns. Nearer at hand, from the open windows of an upper room in the Albergo Centrale came a babble of drunken voices and now and then a shout of laughter. The herrenvolk relaxing, thought the prefetto bitterly, while his fellow citizens cowered in their homes, like small birds when the hawk hovers overhead, waiting to know if to-morrow they would carry out their threat to take hostages and shoot them as a reprisal for the wrecking of the tunnel and the loss of the troop train.

He was up early after a restless night, and by eight o'clock was in his room at the prefecture dealing with routine business which, in war time, included the signing or counter-signing of a large number of forms. He and his wife had not discussed the position as they drank their so-called black coffee and ate their slices of sour bread, but she had kissed him before he came out with unaccustomed fervour, and he knew that she had realised that if hostages were taken he might be one of them.

"And I'm not a brave man," he thought. Already he was perspiring and his straggling grey moustache was limp. He started violently when his secretary came in unheard and stood by his chair.

"Major Weiss to see you, signor prefetto," he said tremulously. "He—he seems very angry."

"Corpo di Bacco—" the prefetto laid down his pen and turned in his swivel chair to face the door. He felt confused and unready.

"Tell my wife—no, never mind—"

The major came in quickly, his heavy boots clattering on the marble floor. His high colour was patchy and his pig's eyes bloodshot after his previous nights potations, and he was evidently in a vile temper. He ignored the prefetto's timid greeting and sat on a corner of the writing-table, pushing aside a stack of forms to give himself room.

"I have come to you," he said harshly, "because you are the civil authority so far as there is any in this place. I may tell you that we consider the local conditions very unsatisfactory. There is slackness and worse. Since we have been here we have interrogated people in every social class and have found a marked unwillingness to co-operate. All this will be reported to the highest quarters, who will take appropriate action."

He narrowed his eyes to stare at the sallow, lined face of the middle-aged Italian, the face of a chronic dyspeptic, and seemed satisfied that he was producing the desired effect on that unhappy official.

"Our immediate objective, as you know, was to find out and punish the authors of the recent outrage. We had reason to believe that the saboteurs were parachutists dropped by an English plane just before it crashed. What became of them during the sixteen days that elapsed between the crash and the blowing up of the tunnel? We set about our enquiry, employing all available means. Did you speak?"

The prefetto shook his head. He was remembering the seven men and two women in hospital with sprains, burns and fractured ribs, and the young woman who had taken sublimate after the Germans left her flat, and was now in the mortuary.

Major Weiss resumed. He was in a better temper now, enjoying his companion's discomfort and mounting apprehension.

"We have found no evidence that this man—or these men, for there may have been two of them—were harboured by anyone in the town."

The prefetto sighed, a long sigh of relief. But the major had not finished with him.

"Yesterday, however, our efforts were rewarded. We found a flying suit of British manufacture and other remains of an airman's equipment buried in the woods not a quarter of a mile from a little farm occupied by a charcoal burner and his wife and daughter. These people were at home and they were closely questioned. You probably know them. Donati was the name and they were tenants of the marchese Gualtieri. Their replies were unsatisfactory and their guilt quite obvious, and they were suitably dealt with."

The prefetto suppressed a shudder. He knew the Donatis. His wife bought their charcoal from the old man.

"The marchese's cousin, Silvio Marucci, was with us at the time. We came back to the town, leaving him there, as he was going on to the Villa to see his mother and arrange for the removal of a piano which we needed for a little party we gave last night. I went myself with a lorry to fetch the instrument, but Marucci was not at the Villa and we saw no one but a half-witted old fool of a servant. Marucci, who is quartered with us at the Centrale, acting as our guide and liaison officer, did not come to the party. We missed him." Weiss smiled unpleasantly. "The little devil could be very amusing. This morning, while I was dressing, I realised that my gold wrist-watch was missing. I remembered looking at the time just after we found the flying suit so I had it on then. It occurred to me that it might have fallen or been wrenched off my wrist while we were examining our prisoners at the farm. It was quite likely. The girl had struggled. A magnificent creature. A young Juno. A pity really. But I digress." The metallic voice clacked on. "My wrist-watch. I sent my orderly, Hans, to the farm to look for it. He came back half an hour ago. Luckily he had found it. The glass is cracked but otherwise it seems uninjured. He also found the body of Silvio Marucci lying in the yard with a fractured skull."

The prefetto's jaw dropped. "But—" he began and checked himself.

Weiss was not listening. "You see now why I have come to you. This is a crime. This is murder. As a matter of courtesy between allies we shall associate you with our search for the criminal. We shall begin our enquiry at the Villa, and you will accompany us. Bring someone who can take notes."

The prefetto licked his dry lips. "My secretary—"

They went down to the waiting car, collecting the secretary on the way. Weiss sat in front beside the wooden-faced Hans, who was driving, and they were followed by a second car packed with men. Gozzoli, the secretary, looked bewildered. He had no idea where they were going or why. The prefetto kept his head down. He was wondering what his fellow townsmen would think when they saw him on the back seat of the major's Opel. He, too, was confused by the turn of events. He had heard what the warder had to tell him when he arrived at the prefecture. Marucci had called at the prison in his own car a little past eleven o'clock and had taken Alda Olivieri away with him. How was it that his body had been found in the yard of the Donati farm a few hours later? There was no road up to it for a car, and the place had already been visited and its occupants dealt with during the previous afternoon. How did he come by the head injuries he must have received before he came to the prison? The warder had referred to his bandages. Was it possible that the Germans themselves had killed him in a drunken quarrel and were now planning to put the blame on someone else?

Whatever the truth the prefetto realised that his own position was precarious. He whispered to his secretary under cover of Hans' heavy-handed changing of gears: "You have come to take notes. Say as little as possible. Know nothing."

The gates at the end of the avenue were closed but not locked. One of the storm troopers in the second car got out and opened them. The road which a month ago had been white with the fallen petals from the acacias in flower was still white with dust which rose about them in clouds. It was very hot. The grounds looked parched and the leaves on the trees were withering. They stopped, with a squealing of brakes, at the main entrance. Hans, at a word from the major, sounded his horn three times. There was no reply to the summons.

Weiss got out and stood with his thick legs apart and his hands on his hips staring up at the long shuttered façade. "Where's that old fool? Is he deaf? Ring the bell, Hans. Knock on the door."

Hans rang and knocked without result.

The major turned abruptly on the two Italians who had joined him. "Marucci was coming here to see his mother yesterday afternoon. When I came to fetch the piano the servant told us the signora had gone to Rome, taking a suitcase, and he did not know when she would return. I thought nothing of it at the time, but it seems odd that she did not inform her son. They appeared to be on excellent terms, and he visited her frequently. This is a very strange affair, signor prefetto. Someone murdered young Marucci. But who? There was no one up in those woods. We had just searched them. Marucci himself went through the house. The Donati couple and their daughter had expiated their crime in harbouring an enemy and had been rendered harmless. In a word they were dead. We met nobody on our way back to the town. One can hardly avoid the conclusion that the killer must have come up from the Villa. What do you say?"

The prefetto, seeing that an answer was expected, was horrified to hear himself saying: "Which killer?"

Luckily Weiss took this as merely another instance of the Italian provincial official's crass stupidity and ignored

it. They stood by helplessly while he barked a series of
orders to his men. Some of them dispersed to search the
grounds. The others waited while Hans broke the glass of
one of the ground-floor windows with a stone and then,
when he had unlatched it, followed the major and the two
Italians as they entered.

Weiss looked about him at the walls panelled with faded
green silk and hung with pale water-colours of a bygone day.

"This is the only room I have seen. Donna Amalia received
us here. A charming woman. Charming. I hope it will not fall
to me to inform her of this outrage. The piano stood there.
How many rooms were normally in use, signor prefetto?
You should know. Marucci told me you were making some
enquiries here lately in connection with the death of the
marchesina."

"Seven bedrooms. The marchese sits in the library when
he is here. Then there is the dining-room, this room, which
the marchesina preferred. That is probably her work basket
with the unfinished piece of embroidery, and the piano was
hers. Donna Amalia had her own sitting-room at the end
of the corridor."

"Such a waste of room would not be allowed in the Reich.
Our Führer would have ordered the owner to make over the
building for some good purpose, holiday quarters for the
Hitler youth, perhaps."

The men had dispersed and could be heard clattering
along corridors, and up and down stairs, opening and shutting doors, breaking, in the unused wing, the silence of
centuries.

The two Italians waited uneasily within a few feet of
the window by which they had entered. Weiss went round
the room peering at the pictures. "I know nothing of these

things," he complained. "They may be valuable. How is one to tell? I can't clutter up the car with useless lumber, but one does not like to feel one may be missing something."

The prefetto's eyes bulged as the German pushed a sofa out from the wall to get a closer view of a portrait in pastels. He had seen a reddish-brown stain on the carpet which the sofa had concealed. Would the major notice it? "Blood," he thought. "Something happened here yesterday." He glanced at Gozzoli and saw that he was frightened. But Weiss, luckily, had a one-track mind and for the moment his attention was concentrated on the pictures, wondering whether they were worth taking. His plump, practical flaxen-haired wife had warned him that there was no room in their Munich flat for junk.

"I don't think they're up to much," he decided, and casually shoved the sofa back to its former position.

The prefetto took out his handkerchief and wiped his forehead.

A young S.S. trooper came in, saluted, and made his report. Weiss translated for the prefetto's benefit.

"He says he found the old manservant in the kitchen. There's no one else in the place. Bring him in, Streicher. We'll see what we can get out of him."

Pietro came in between two troopers, but the prefetto noticed that they were not holding him. He bowed, not to anyone in particular but in their direction, a bow that was a miracle of tact, and said; *"Buon giorno, signori,"* and waited respectfully for their orders.

Weiss glowered at him. "Why didn't you come to the door? You must have heard us."

"I am sorry, signore. The truth is I am deaf, a little deaf. When my wife is here she hears the bell and tells me, but she has gone to nurse her sister who is very ill and I am alone here."

"When did she go?"

"Yesterday morning, signore, soon after Donna Amalia left. Donna Amalia gave her leave."

Weiss grunted. "Did you have any visitors during the day?"

"No, signore."

"Young Marucci. I know you told me yesterday you had not seen him, but perhaps he came later, after I had fetched away the piano. Be careful. Do not lie to me. You will regret it if you do. We have ways and means of getting at the truth."

"If he came, signore, it was without my knowledge. He might come and go again without my hearing him. He is at home here. He is one of the family."

The trooper who had come in last evidently understood Italian and was following the trend of the examination. He was very young, not more than nineteen, with a round, red face and eyes as hard as grey pebbles. He seemed to be privileged for he had taken up his position behind Weiss' chair where he lounged at his ease, and interjected an occasional comment in an undertone meant only for the major's ear.

Weiss listened, frowning. "Is that so? That is strange." He raised his voice. "Marucci had his car here in the garage. It is gone. What has become of it?"

"I do not know, signore. Two men came last night and took it away."

"Is that so?" Weiss spoke now with a false geniality that was more threatening than the bull-like roar with which he had begun his interrogation. "Why didn't you say so before?"

"You said during the day, signore. This was late in the evening."

"Who were these men?"

"They were strangers to me. They said they were members of the OVRA, the secret police. They showed me papers with seals and the signature of the Duce."

The prefetto, trembling inwardly at his own temerity, intervened for the first time. "Isn't it possible that Marucci's death was due to disciplinary action taken by OVRA? Such things are not unknown."

"It's an idea," said Weiss. He was obviously impressed by the suggestion. "What do you think, Siegfried?"

The young trooper grinned. "It might be. He never took me in. I always knew your golden-haired pet was a double-crossing rat. And sooner or later rats get caught in traps. A good riddance, I say."

Weiss pushed back his chair. "Well, I really think—" he began in a much milder tone. The prefetto felt sure that he was about to say that they had wasted quite enough time over the enquiry and that it might be regarded as closed as far as the German military authorities were concerned. But another trooper came in before he could finish what he was going to say. There was another quick interchange of guttural German. Weiss rapped out an order and the two men who had brought Pietro into the room moved closer to him and gripped his wrists, one on each side. He looked quickly from one to the other and his lips moved but he made no sound.

Weiss turned to the prefetto and said formally: "My men have found something in the garden. We had better see for ourselves. Come, signor prefetto."

The french window was opened and they all passed out, including the prisoner and his escort, and, crossing the terrace where, earlier in the summer, Donna Amalia and the two girls had sat each evening drinking their coffee and watching the moon rise, went, by way of the lily pool, down the ilex walk to the kitchen garden.

The prefetto realised that for some time he had been hearing the excited yapping of a dog, interrupted at intervals by a sharp howl as if someone was trying to silence the animal with a kick.

Several of the troopers were standing together by a piece of ground that had been recently dug up and neatly raked over. One of the troopers stepped forward. He was holding a large yellow mongrel on a lead made of a bit of old rope. The poor beast looked half-starved, its ribs showed through its skin. Its muzzle and paws were smeared with earth.

The trooper pointed to the untidy beginnings of a hole in the loose soil. There was no need to speak. The major bent over the hole. After a minute he beckoned to the prefetto who joined him reluctantly.

"Someone has been buried here, but not deep enough. A woman. Black silk with a pattern of white butterflies. An unusual pattern. Donna Amalia was wearing a dress of that material when we called here three days ago." He turned away and signed to the escort to bring forward their prisoner. "Hold out his hands. No. Palms upward. Look, signor prefetto, at the blisters. He's an indoor servant, not used to digging. This, I think, is a matter for the local authorities."

The prefetto cleared his throat. He looked very unhappy. "Have you anything to say, Pietro?"

The old man's faded blue eyes met his without flinching. "I was always sure that la Marucci poisoned Donna Chiara, but I could not prove it. I knew no one would listen to me, and justice must be done, so I shot her and buried her. That is the gardener's dog. Please do not hurt him. He meant no harm."

Chapter XXI
HE WILL COME BACK

They entered Rome just as day was breaking. The journey had been uneventful. They had been stopped twice, but Silvio's permit cut through war-time restrictions. Richard only grunted in reply to questions and the marchese spoke for him, explaining that he was suffering from facial injuries that made any attempt to speak difficult and painful.

It was still very early when the car stopped at the door of the Convent in the Via Due Macelli. Richard pulled off the bandages that swathed his head and face. They had served their purpose and would only attract attention now. He got out and rang the bell before he helped Caterina to alight. He turned quickly as she crossed the pavement with the sleeping baby in her arms, and seeing that Alda was numbed and stiff after the long drive he lifted her out. For a moment they clung together in silence before their lips met. He was suddenly and profoundly happy.

"She's sweet," he thought. "I was right. This is it, the real thing." When he got back into the driving seat his face was white. The marchese, who had remained in the car, glanced at him and looked away again.

Richard made an effort to control his voice. "Where to now, sir?"

"My house in the Piazza Navona. Don't worry. She will be safe with the nuns."

"Yes, I know." He let in the clutch.

In the afternoon of the following day the marchese Gualtieri came to the convent to visit his sister, the Reverend Mother Superior. He asked the lay sister who showed him into the parlour if he might see the signorina Olivieri first for a few minutes.

Alda did not keep him waiting long. The nuns had provided her with a black frock and her brown curls were combed back and tied with ribbon. She looked very young.

Gualtieri took her hand and led her to a chair. "Sit down, *cara*. You are rested?"

"Yes, thank you."

"Were you frightened when you were brought out of the prison?"

"At first, when I thought you were the OVRA, yes. But when you stopped to pick up Caterina outside the Villa gates she explained it all. The baby is well," she added, "they are giving him goat's milk."

He nodded. "The Reverend Mother will take care of him—and of you." He hesitated. "I hope you have forgiven me, Alda."

"Forgiven you?" She looked at him uncertainly. "For what?"

"I was too ready to believe a thing that should have appeared incredible—that you were responsible for Chiara's death. I—I—" he struggled with his pride—"I have been punished for my blindness, my folly. The innocent—I shall never forgive myself," he said bitterly.

He seemed an old and broken man, no longer formidable and Alda felt sorry for him. "It was not your fault," she said impulsively. "La Marucci was very clever."

"You know that she is dead?"

"Caterina told me."

"Did she tell you how she died?"

"No. I did not ask. I do not want to think about her—or Silvio." She shuddered. "They were horrible."

"Very well," he said. "I hope you will be able to forget. Perhaps in different surroundings, another country—I have a message for you from your Englishman."

She said quickly; "Where is he now? Is he safe?"

"I hope so. I tried to persuade him to enter the Vatican City and be interned, but he would not. There is, it seems, an underground movement here in Rome which assists allied airmen, and either hides them or enables them to make their way back to their own lines. He spent yesterday with me in my flat in the Piazza Navona, and left us after dark. He told us where he wanted to go and Nicolo set him on his way, and I induced him to accept a little money to help him on the journey."

"You said there was a message?"

"He said: Please tell her that if I am alive when this is over I shall come back. She knows how I feel. I shall not change."

"Thank you," she said quietly.

"It is an extraordinary affair," said the marchese reflectively. "But I like him. I think you might do worse. I hope you will remain here in my sister's care to wait for him. Will you do that? I may not have another opportunity to advise you."

"I should be very glad. The Mother Superior has been very kind."

"Good." He took her hand again and looked down at her earnestly. "You are a good little girl. My son, I know, thought highly of you, and you were a loyal friend to poor Chiara. God bless you, my dear. Goodbye."

When his sister came in a few minutes later she looked at him searchingly. "What did you say to the child to make her cry?"

"Nothing. Was she crying? Sit down, Virginia. I want to talk to you."

She had always been proud of him, always admired him. He held himself erect as ever, but it seemed to her that in ten days he had aged by as many years. She said: "Are you leaving your grandson with us?"

"If you will have him."

"I shall have to ask permission, but I think it will be given. Something more has happened. Caterina would have talked, but I would not listen. You shall tell me as much as you think it right I should know."

"Very well. You will have guessed that I should not have brought Alda to you if I had not become convinced of her innocence. Virginia, I shall never forgive myself. I made my own life here, doing the historical research work that has been my main interest, reading, writing, having shifted my domestic responsibilities to shoulders that seemed more fitted to bear them. I had—you have heard me say it—the utmost confidence in the Marucci. She saved me trouble, so I did not look too closely," he said, his voice bitter with self-contempt. "Virginia, I know for certain now that she poisoned Chiara. Chiara was in correspondence with a couple she and Amedeo met during their honeymoon, these people knew Amalia's true character. She and her son were notorious in Venice. Amalia must have found one of their letters or overheard something that made her realise that Chiara must be silenced before she came to me. That is not all. She nursed my wife during the last phase of her illness.

Perhaps my poor Lucia too was her victim. I cannot be sure, but I suspect."

"Has she been arrested? Was your evidence sufficient?"

"I went directly to Menotti—he is the prefetto now—he told me quite frankly that he dared not move in the matter. The woman's son was a hanger-on of the Fascist Grand Council, and had made himself very useful to the Germans. He was known to be a member of the secret police."

The nun sat with her folded hands hidden by the long loose sleeves of her habit. Her thin face, ivory pale, with her brother's clear-cut profile, was carefully inexpressive. Years of self-repression had armed her against any onslaught on her emotions.

"What did you do?"

He was silent for a moment. Then he said: "She is dead."

"I see." She looked at him steadily. "I will have masses said for her soul. The sisters and I will pray."

"Her soul is damned in hell, but pray by all means, my dear, if it gives you any satisfaction. You may like to include the name of her son in your petitions. He was killed at about the same time, but I had no hand in that affair. He and his German friends had just shot the Donati family, the old couple and Marietta, and Silvio was trying to set fire to the house with my grandson in it. What is the matter?"

She had covered her face with her hands. She looked up at him now. "All this blood and violence. God help us. It is like a bad dream. When shall we wake?"

"All this has been a shock," he said more gently. "I am sorry you had to know, but it was necessary. I am leaving Alda Olivieri with you. She has had a romance with a young English airman who has been hiding in our woods. He may come back for her some day."

"You approve?"

"Certainly. He saved the life of my grandson. That is a debt I can never repay, but I have done all I can. If he is not caught and shot as a spy before he rejoins his friends, if he does not crash on land or fall into the sea—if he is more fortunate than Amedeo—she will not wait in vain, I think. His name, by the way, is Richard Drew. But you will hear all about him, no doubt, from her," he added with his faint smile.

She had recovered her composure. Her hands were hidden again in her sleeves and he could not see them trembling. She could hear the splashing of the fountain in the courtyard, that sound of running water that is the authentic voice of Rome. There was something final about all this. She felt it. She said: "Very well. But what are your own plans?"

"I made a new will this morning. I had to provide for my grandson and for Alda, and, of course, for the servants, Nicolo here, and Pietro and his wife at the Villa."

"You have done—and will do—what you think right," she said.

"Yes." He made a perceptible effort and went on without looking at her. "Just now, on my way here, at the barber's, I picked up this morning's paper. You don't know what journalism is like to-day, my dear sister. Incredibly melodramatic and vulgar. I saw the headlines. *Another macabre discovery at the fatal Villa. Sinister aftermath of the Gualtieri poisoning affair.* The body of Amalia Marucci has been found buried in the garden. Pietro was questioned and made a full confession of his guilt."

"Pietro?"

"His story is that he was convinced that she murdered Chiara but thought it could never be proved, so he took the law into his own hands."

"And is that the truth?"

"Of course not. I killed her. The dear old man is lying out of loyalty to the family. I am going back to Mont Alvino now to give myself up. So we are not likely to meet again in this life, Virginia. Try to think of me kindly."

She rose swiftly, laid her hands on his shoulders, and kissed him on both cheeks. "My poor brother," she said indistinctly. "I shall pray for you."

After he had gone she went into the chapel and knelt in her usual place in the choir, looking towards the altar where the sanctuary lamp glimmered like a red star in the incense-scented gloom. The noises of the street did not penetrate here, but now and then there was a rumble as of distant thunder, the voice of the guns, louder now than yesterday as the tide of war flowed towards Rome. She was aware of Alda, kneeling too, in the place of the novices. But Alda, she thought, would never take the veil. She was young, there would be light for her at the end of the dark tunnel. For Alda there was still hope.

THE END

KINDRED SPIRITS . . .

Why not join the

DEAN STREET PRESS
FACEBOOK GROUP

for lively bookish chat
and more

Scan the QR code below

Or follow this link
**www.facebook.com/groups/
deanstreetpress**

Ingram Content Group UK Ltd.
Milton Keynes UK
UKHW041342160423
420245UK00001B/241